ROUGH PATCH

ROUGH PATCH

NICOLE MARKOTIĆ

ARSENAL PULP PRESS
VANCOUVER

ARSENAL PULP PRESS
Suite 202 – 211 East Georgia St.
Vancouver, BC V6A 1Z6
Canada
arsenalpulp.com

The publisher gratefully acknowledges the support of the Canada Council for the Arts
and the British Columbia Arts Council for its publishing program, and the Government
of Canada (through the Canada Book Fund) and the Government of British Columbia
(through the Book Publishing Tax Credit Program) for its publishing activities.

This is a work of fiction. Any resemblance of characters to persons either living or deceased is
purely coincidental.

Cover and text design by Oliver McPartlin
Edited by Susan Safyan

Printed and bound in Canada

Library and Archives Canada Cataloguing in Publication:

Marcotić, Nicole, author
    Rough patch / Nicole Marcotić.

Issued in print and electronic formats.
ISBN 978-1-55152-681-2 (softcover).--ISBN 978-1-55152-682-9
(HTML)

    I. Title.

PS8626.A735R68 2017   jC813'.6   C2017-900682-7
                                       C2017-900683-5

for Suzette Mayr: bff & f & f
(thru thick & thru all-things-gerbil)

PROLOGUE

Hello! My name is Keira, and I'm bisexual ... ☺

Don't you think high school would be a lot easier if we all had nametags that blared our true selves? I imagine wearing this nametag as I glide onto the skating rink, first thing this early, early September morning (pre-morning for most people), the ice pristine and non-judgmental and virginal. The air smells like baked cloves and mint and the Ice Capades, which (dork alert) I used to beg my parents to take me to. I haven't been on the ice for a month, and my body misses the shivery chill and goose pimples I get along my arms to my shoulders. Coach won't be here till tomorrow morning; today is just warm-up. So why am I shivering? I'm nervous that having been away will skewer my chances at winning anything this year. But my feet remember this early-morning routine. I skate out to a smooth patch, long easy strides, because my body knows what to do. On the ice, that is—no clue how to navigate the first day of high school. Today. If I wore this actual nametag, it'd be a way of getting myself out there, without having to explain, well, *everything*.

Yeah, right.

Wearing this nametag would pretty much be the demise of high school as I know it, and I don't even know it yet! The first day of classes would turn into the last. Finito. The End. Shortest memoir in history: I wore a nametag to school, announced my deviant sexual orientation to every teen I passed in the halls, and was then transferred to a fundamentalist reform school where the rumour was that I was a big lesbo but the kids mainly left me alone because, hell, I was already headed there. At this thought, my left foot wobbles, and I nick my first flaw onto this flat sheet of polished ice.

Let me try again: My name is Keira. I'm fifteen years old, live in Alberta, have a mom who micromanages too much of her kids' lives, a dad who's really lenient (except for those times when he's not), a little sister Samantha—Sam to me—who I adore, an older brother Tyler, who I don't (more on him later), and today I start grade ten. I have a best friend, Sita, and I love winter, mostly because I'm smitten with figure skating. Oh, yeah, and I'm bisexual. I think. And single, natch.

Figure skating gear is pretty pricey, and I have to pay for extra ice time. I'd like to get some individual coaching, which is expensive, but Mom doesn't want me to work because she thinks having lots of cash will make me think a dead-end job is better than an education. But rather than put it that way, she said, "You're busy enough with school and skating, Keira. I want your focus on studying." Bleh. Still, she agreed to let me take a summer job. And yesterday when they picked me up at the end of my four weeks away, I decided to take the plunge and talk to them about an after-school job. No Tyler in the car, so no bickering between us, and no evidence of bickering between Mom and Dad. I hugged them both and threw my junk in the back seat. Soon as Dad picked up his coffee mug, I burst out, "I want to talk about getting more work."

Red light. They both sipped from their coffee (caffeine in stereo, man). I already cleaned one dentist's place once a week. And he'd told me a gazillion times that he had colleagues who'd hire me on his recommendation alone, but Mom said once a week was pocket money—any more and it'd be a real job. That's what I wanted.

"Listen, I'm finished junior high, and I get okay grades, right?" Start with the highlights. "And I know my skating hobby costs money, but I'm dedicated, yes?" No, I do *not* think skating is a hobby, but you absolutely have to use parent-speak when begging. Green light. Mom put her coffee back in the cup holder; Dad clutched his with both hands.

"Truth be true, I don't want to have to ask you guys every time I need to buy a new pen or ruler for school." Yeah, like that's why I want a job, so I can stock up on school supplies! "So how about we make a deal?" This is the tricky part, because parents *never* like deals. They like making rules and having their kids follow those rules. A deal sounds too much like negotiation. But if you treat them like they're idjits, they retaliate by refusing, no matter *what* you're asking for.

"Hear me out," I said, waving away their unspoken rebuttal, smiling at Mom in the rearview mirror. "You want me to get good grades so I can go to university and get a good job, right?" They didn't even nod; everything I said was so obvious and indisputable. "If—I said *if*—you let me get a job, just a few more shifts a week, I promise I'll get a B or higher in every course. And I will *never* let the job get in the way of studying." I took a breath. This conversation was a one-way street. Maybe broaching this topic in the car wasn't such a good idea. "Best of all, the job will help my goal of getting to university."

Mom studied me for a moment in the rearview mirror. So far, me getting to university has always been *her* goal.

"Your dream is really to clean up other people's spit?" Dad asked. He should talk—he gets paid to get strangers drunk. Who says you have to adore your job to be happy? Here I am, close to sweet sixteen, training in a sport that has *no* career opportunities, and I don't like any subjects at school except math. If Mom has visions of her daughter becoming some high-powered lawyer chick, she is *so* going to be disappointed. I ignored Dad's question and kept talking.

"I promise that half of what I make goes into the bank, into an account I *never* withdraw from, ever. It'll be for tuition, for course books, for whatever they'll charge students by the time I graduate from high school." I took another breath. A big one.

"B?" was all Mom said.

"Okay, B-plus." Except I couldn't promise too much here. I am not a stellar student like Sita. I rolled down the window, then rolled it up again. "Look, I'll occasionally get a lower grade on *some* of the assignments. But at least a B-plus as a *final grade* in every class, okay?" Then I held my breath. Unless I blew my finals, I could usually make a B in all my subjects. I'd have to up my game a bit. Really cram, even for quizzes. And tie pretty bows around take-home assignments. Teachers like it if it looks like you made an extra effort.

"Done," Dad said, before the Mom Police could digest the full extent of my deal, and he rolled down his own window, letting in the end-of-long-weekend traffic racket.

"And no garbage," Mom added, turning into our street. Like I was going to spend my hard-earned cash on e-cigs or nose piercings. Most of it would go to skating—she should know that.

Soon as we got home, I emailed the dentist whose offices I cleaned to tell him I could work on Tuesdays and Thursdays after school and one afternoon over the weekend. I'd have to really zip it to the bus after school, though, cuz dentists don't work late. Mom should go back to dental school. *That* might make her happy! Though does anything ever make Mom happy? Certainly not what she calls my "extra-curricular" gliding, like skating is some sort of bungee-jumping hobby. Skating is just the opposite: when I'm on the ice, I glide through air while slicing across frozen liquid.

SPOILER ALERT: THIS CHICK CAN'T EVEN FIGURE OUT IF SHE WANTS TO KISS A BOY MORE, OR A GIRL—DEFINITELY AN ICE CAPADES QUEEN!

CHAPTER ONE

I'm still going over yesterday's bargain about work and grades at 6:30 in the morning. But I need to focus on the ice now. I pass a sprinkling of other skaters looping their figure 8s, tracing lines that look like the Möbius strips we learned about in math last year. Maybe the goal is to create a perfect symbol of infinity, which explains why we ice geeks get up at the crack of dawn to go round and round and round but never get anywhere. No, not nowhere—as the medals and ribbons that line my wall attest. And this year, Winnie (yes, that's my coach's real name) has talked my parents into letting me compete nationally. I'm gearing up for the Regionals here in town and the Provincials in January (in Alberta for once!), with smaller Wild Rose and Silver Ice competitions in between, then the Nationals in April. Winnie has mentioned the World Championships, depending on how I do in the Nationals, which does make me sweat a bit, even on the ice.

I shiver again, then scrape a small X with the heel of my skate and begin to etch out my first figure 8. I'd rather leap right into the leaps and jumps, but practicing balance and precision makes sense first thing in the morning, especially since I've been away for four weeks. Makes a lot of sense, especially with a body as ungainly off the ice as mine can be: I'm tall and thin, but with thick leg muscles. And now I'm thinking about my bi-quest all over again: I'm itching to lust after someone who lusts after tall and thin, but strong. You'd think lusting after all kinds of bodies would generate a little action.

You'd be wrong. Except for one exceptional lip-lock in August, I am still pretty much a virginal cliché.

I like boys; I like girls. There were about seventeen girls and three boys in my last school that I would have liked to kiss. About twenty more of each that I was willing to kiss. But none of them would kiss me back. Well, maybe "back" isn't exactly the right word. In order to kiss me back, I would first have had to actually tried to kiss one of them ... maybe at a junior high dance, when the chaperones were out sneaking smokes, or at a drunken party where the parents had retreated upstairs and the lights had pretty much disappeared. Never happened. In fact, I have yet to snog a single schoolmate, male or female. Why? Um, because I'm a second-rate homo and a first-rate coward? Because, at some point, I'd have to *explain* myself?

Of course, I wouldn't *have* to explain anything. I could let Sita match me up with a boy and go on merrily (what, you want me to say "gaily"?) dating him until we broke up for some dumb reason, like he forgot our second-month anniversary (by the way "anni" means year—you cannot have a monthly-yearly—I googled it during Life Skills class) or because I didn't like his friends always dragging him off to play World4War when we should've been kissing. Simple—no mention of girls, no mention of how my body is, like, *conflicted*, and could he just be patient while I worked the whole thing out.

Again and again, I trace the number 8 with my feet. Circle, cross, circle, cross: an even number and a mirror of itself. Or, I could kiss a girl. I really wanna kiss a girl. Yeah, yeah, you're thinking, this chick's just a big fat lez who doesn't want to come out, so she's invented the bisexual story to cover up her true lust and hide, just a little, behind "normal." Sigh. Your reaction is almost entirely exactly why I don't tell anyone, not even the gay kids at school (*especially* not the gay kids), that I am a by-sex-you-all. Even after a month up in the boonies at my summer job (more on that later), skating practice feels like the most normal thing I do. After I'm done with my figures, I practice spins and toe loops and a Lutz. But not an Axel jump yet; I'll need way more time on the ice before I'm totally up to speed.

Yes, I would like to kiss a girl, maybe get a girlfriend. But I would, after said kiss, have a lot of explaining to do. More so than with a boy, cuz judging from my limited experience, boys don't really want to talk and analyze and describe and examine and then talk some more. I'm thinking that if you're a fifteen-year-old girl and so together that you've figured out you're a lesbian *and* come out at school *and* found another girl to kiss, well, you don't want your girlfriend going on and on about how she still likes boys, right?

I spent most of the last two years staring at girls' chests and boys' shoulders. Come summer in Alberta, girls wear really low-cut tops and boys usually go shirtless. And I find myself drinking it all in. Secretly, of course—at least the boobs. But even staring at boys can get a het-girl in trouble. Girls are supposed to be sexy and tuned in to whatever guys have in mind, but we're also supposed to be cute about it, following the guy's lead, like this isn't the twenty-first century. As girls, though, we lust quite lustily through our teen years as much as boys do.

Sita's been bugging me to release myself from the skating squad and join the dating squad instead, but I've been dragging my ice picks, so to speak. Sita has never been a big fan of my skating life, especially when it intrudes on after-school hang-out times. But—finally!—I have news for Sita about this summer, news she'll want to hear, but I still don't know how to tell her—*that's* how mixed up I am. That's the problem with being bisexual—you have to kiss either boys or girls all the time, or everyone thinks you're just a poser. Am I a poser? Does needing to prepare myself for a chat with my best friend prove it?

All the other skaters at the rink this morning except one are girls, and we're covered neck to ankles. No fancy competition regalia so early in fall, just jackets light enough to let us move, dense enough to hug us warm during frigid practices. Still, under all those layers are sports bras and one jock strap and maybe even frilly panties. Picturing underwear and bare skin in this frosty space multiplies my chills. I shake my arms and legs and then glide around a small area to practice my camel spins. I lean my body forward, trying to stay parallel, with one leg straight out behind me. Not usually difficult for me, but I'm out of shape, and my balance is off.

"Go ahead," Winnie had said, when I told her about my plan to miss a month of skate practice.

"I'll do stretches every morning," I promised. "And as many jump-squats as you assign!"

"No, I mean it: go ahead," she repeated, and this time I couldn't hear sarcasm in her voice. "Sometimes a break allows the body to remember in different ways." She raised one eyebrow, which is her way of winking. "You wanna go hiking and camping, I'm not gonna stand in your way, and it could actually help in the long run, s'long as you practice jumps and squat exercises every day." She paused, considering adding some sit-spins to my summer mornings, then concluded, "I recommend a two-week break, but a superstar like you can manage twice that." She raised the other eyebrow. Maybe a little sarcasm? "Not like you're off chasing after boys."

Allow me a short tangent, cuz I need to rant: You're a teen and beginning to work out that, well, you get turned on a lot. Easy for boys—everyone expects them to be turned on, by everyone and everything. Once I was watching a *Kids in the Hall* rerun (the '90s really crack me up) and in the skit, Scott Thompson was doing his recurring character of "Buddy," queen icon extraordinaire. (Yeah, a gay guy playing a gay guy—how's that for layered?) Anyway, I don't remember the plot, but Buddy was going on and on about how he'd been sexed up by a fancy chair, turned on by its exquisite lines and sensual stance. Hilarious—because he's gay, and all gay people think about is sex? Or because he's a guy, and all guys think about is sex?

But girls are supposed to fend off the hordes of boys trampling each other to get us into bed. Where *are* these hordes? Oh, I admit that more guys are out there pressuring girls into the sack than the other way around, but the story absolutely everyone still believes is that girls don't need sex. Except for nymphos. Girls supposedly wait for the boy train to make a stop at their station. Really fair, huh? About as fair as being gay in a straight world. Think about it: how many kids have to gather their parents into a sports-like huddle and "confess" that they're attracted to the opposite sex? "Mom, Dad, hear me out, I'm straight. I know you're disappointed, but ..." Yeah, like when has *that* conversation ever taken place?

Okay, end of rant.

My leggings are coated with ice from the rink, but my muscles are so warm my knees tingle. Except for the past few weeks of summer, I do skate practice at 6:30 every morning, five days a week. For me, there's no, *Let's just play this sport for fun once a month or so.* You're either serious about heading for every skating competition within affordable range, or you're only lacing up the figure skates every December for the holidays. No middle ground in ice skating, no in-between. Which, as I step out of the rink and head away from the one place in the world I feel comfortable in my body, brings me back to my personal quest of trying to survive high school along with my aberrant "in-between" lust.

My stomach bounces around, not sure whether to be more nervous about the first day of high school, my body's bifurcated longings (bi-forking, get it?), or finally having that big talk with Sita. A quick three-turn, and I speed backward around the rink, looking behind me over my shoulder. Done in, I collapse onto the benches, my stiff fingers fumbling to undo my skates. The laces seem fused together and my gloves are drenched with ice crystals clinging to the finger tips. My heart's beating a tune along with the terrible music crackling through the speakers. I'm totally starving, with only minutes to get home, scarf down breakfast, and rush off to pick up Sita on our way to senior high. Gulp, first day of high school. Did I mention my idea for everyone wearing nametags to proclaim our sexual orientation? I'd wither into a stalk of thirty-week-old celery if I had to wear a nametag announcing *anything* about my sexuality at school. Or anywhere. I don't want to shout out loud and proud, I want to hide away, hushed and shushed. The nametag idea is—I am almost too wretched to even admit this—for *me*. Because *I* don't know what I want. Who I want. Who I want to be when I'm wanting.

LESBO ALERT: SHE NEVER TOUCHES A CURLING IRON.

HET-GIRL ALERT: SHE LACES HER CANVAS SNEAKERS WITH GAUDY RIBBONS.

CHAPTER TWO

All summer I've been pining for a great chat with my best friend, Sita. We spent four weeks apart and finally get to see each other on this, the first day of school. Today. I am a bundle of excitement and terror and jiggly breakfast granola (why didn't I skip a meal, just this once?). Soon as I see Sita, I'm going to tell her all about Surge. My brother calls his best friend Hurler, and the first boy I kiss has the guy-fuelled nickname Surge. He could talk about boring hockey statistics all summer, but then lean closer as an elder braided three strands of sweet grass during a cultural awareness training session. And when she told him that sweet grass is the sacred hair of Mother Earth, his forehead wrinkled into a thousand smiles. I grab my bag, toss a wave at Sam, whoosh out the front door, and walk to my best friend's while rehearsing, rehearsing, rehearsing. "Keira, give me the haps!" she'll shout as she rushes into my arms. And I'll dive in: "Sita, in the last days of summer, I ... well, the forest isn't all gophers and badgers, you know. Let's just say my lips aren't virgins any more."

But when I reach her yard, before I can say a thing, she bursts out the door and screams: "Keira, I kissed Lucien! A grade twelve boy!" So much for my great timing. Sita is adorable, whereas I'm ... okay, I guess. I have short hair, short-short but not buzzed. I wear lipstick sometimes, but I never wear heels cuz I'm pretty tall already. Sita is just pretty, period. Her hair smells of cinnamon and falls just below her shoulders, though she sometimes ties it up in elaborate twists and braid-loops. She has a cute nose, cute chin, and always wears dangly earrings that show off her cute earlobes. Her eyes crinkle when she laughs, and making her laugh is the greatest feeling, ever. She's laughing now cuz we haven't see each other in *eons*.

I have *big* news and Sita has stolen my moment. Our hug lasts and lasts, but I'm also sorta miffed. For the first time in the history of our friendship, I have kissing news. But naturally, Sita has bigger news. Hug ends and we speed-walk to school, Sita offering me her new-boy details. "How'd you get a date before school even started?" I ask as we head toward the big bad.

"Not a date, just a couple of kissing sessions." Sita's wearing a baby blue scarf that matches her shoes and her belt. I watch her lips as she talks and they seem excited, if that's possible. Do my lips look different? Do my clothes count as matching if shirt, skirt, and sneakers are all pretty much washed-out tan? As we enter the school grounds, I slow our pace. We're not late, and I have zero interest in being early. Slowing down will give me a chance to think. Better to make my confession after school, I decide, when we'll have more time.

Sita doesn't share my restraint. "I ran into Lucien downtown last week. You know, the mall with that indoor-outdoor garden on the top floor? He was actually shopping for school supplies with his mother, if you can believe it, though they were deep in disagreement about the definition of what counts as proper grade twelve goods." Sita talks in paragraphs without breathing.

Then she offers up details about Lucien and his "luscious lips." I let her tell me all about how he likes the way her fingers taper down to her fingertips (yep, he said "taper"). Soon as they managed a mom-less meeting, they kissed and groped a bit but mainly just locked lips and held hands. "Lucien doesn't want to date. He wants to be free in his last year of school," Sita says and does this wave of her hand, dismissing my objections before I even get to say them. "I know, I know, he thinks dating somehow steals his freedom. He's a boy, what do you expect?"

"I expect him not to kiss you when no one's around then just dump you as soon as school starts!" Sita's the one always advising me to demand a lot, never to settle. One kiss from this Lucien guy, and all her boy-lessons go out the window, kaplooey?

"He didn't dump me. He said right from the beginning that we weren't doing the dating thing." And then she actually gets a dreamy look on her face! "Just the kissing thing."

"He's a jerk," I tell her. But Sita does her hand-wave gesture at me. "Of *course* he's a jerk, that's why *I'm* not gonna date *him*." The dreamy look again. "But it was mind-blowing kissing, and now I'm the one who's free to date a boy I actually like talking to."

So: they have to be good at kissing *and* talking. Tall order.

"Do *not* worry," she reassures me as we enter the school grounds, "we'll have you dating senior boys in no time flat!"

Smokers crowd around the side door, jocks crowd the fields, and a wall of faces I've never seen stare out at us. Lots of girls in flared skirts, like we've re-invented the '50s. Where are all the kids from last year? Four junior high schools feed into this high school. I should recognize *somebody*, but every face is new. And seems hostile.

Since she's filled me in on the Lucien details and the bell's about to ring, Sita demands I sum up the best and the worst of the summer, in one sentence each.

"Best: no parents and lots of outdoorsy fun." Short and sweet, but—coward that I am—leaving out the *best* best part. "And worst: mosquitoes, mosquitoes, mosquitoes." I take a gulp of breath. Should I dive back in, redo my one-sentence summaries? But we're surrounded by students clustering around the entranceway. Sita considers the wall of strangers. "Hey, look, there's Amanda. Oh, and Marisol. And there's Raf heading inside. Let's go."

And not to get too biblical or anything, but the wall parts and we nudge past the strangers through the double doors to where the halls teem with kids who look way older and way cooler than I'll ever be. "Hmph." Sita sounds disappointed. "Lockers, crammed classrooms, and graffiti. Welcome to the brand-new same-old."

We check our schedules and—groan—we don't even have lunch together. Tuesday (today, two other dentists hired me already!) and Thursday afternoons, I have to burn off to my after-school job. Wednesday will be Drama Club for Sita, so I'll have to wait till Friday. This is how Sita and I operate. We need a whole afternoon of just us, of catching up on vital and extensive gossip.

Sita shunts us over to the office so we can get our locker assignments. The secretaries don't come across as mean exactly, but they're not super friendly either. One keeps banging a sheaf of papers onto the counter to punctuate her instructions: "Locker number 1437 ..." *bang* "Go right at the stairwell near where Yearbook meets." *bang* "Fourth floor." *bang* "You can remember that because of the four in fourteen." If we need directions to our own lockers, how're we supposed to know where Yearbook Club meets? "Locker number 1722 ..." *bang* "Go past the second gym and up to the second floor." *bang*

"No, second, not seventh." *bang* "If the combos don't work, check your locker number before coming back down here. Check three times."

Guess this can't be their favourite week of the year. Maybe coming back to school to *work* is a worse bummer than having to come as a student? As we exit the office, Sita whispers, "I am going to *try* to forgive you for abandoning me over the summer," but since she doesn't know about Dianne and Surge, it's a joke threat. I do, truly, want to tell her my summer secrets; I don't just want to tell her *one* thing about myself, but *both* things: bi-things. And for that, my timing needs to be perfect. Friday.

HET-GIRL ALERT: AFRAID THAT IF SHE TELLS HER BEST FRIEND ABOUT DIANNE, SHE'LL GET LABELLED A LESBO, FOR SURE.

LESBO ALERT: AFRAID THAT IF SHE TELLS HER BEST FRIEND ABOUT SURGE, SHE'LL JUST BE DEAD STRAIGHT, NO GIRL FANTASIES ALLOWED.

CHAPTER THREE

Summers, my family never does anything besides camping, and only for a bunch of three-day clumps when my parents can coordinate their holidays. Total family-focus. In other words: dull. But Sammie really gets off on planning those trips. Maybe because she doesn't have to do physio on vacation, or maybe because her wheelchair is just so fascinating to other campers. This past summer, she made a cardboard sign reading, "No fee for photos." And held it up, adding sweetly, "although monetary gifts are always appreciated." Dad took away the sign and let anyone take as many photos as they wanted, with him in the photo posing as if he's on the verge of lifting her and her chair.

So last spring, we were up in the room we share, planning the summer holidays. I could easily see Sammie growing up to be a general. She's covered the walls on her side with maps and old-timey drawings made to look like photos: a bird mid-flight, a half-submerged alligator yawning in a swamp. Our mom constructed a lap-desk to fit Sammie's chair so it can hold all her school supplies. Mostly, Sammie stuffs the chair's many pockets with her explorer magazines, stickers, card games, and joke books. To prep, she hauled out two different topographic maps. "We'll start out in Banff," she announced, "curve down into Montana, then up through Washington, across the BC Rockies, and end up in Jasper." She hunched over the map, slapping on stickies every 400 km or so.

"Remember," I asked her, "that one place where we dared Tyler to jump off the cliff and he did, and then we *all* got into trouble?" Sammie adores our puke of an older brother, but that doesn't stop her from doing her best to get him into trouble. Even when she sometimes has to pay a price herself.

"Kiki, this time, we won't *dare* him to jump, we'll *warn* him *not* to!" Sammie cracks me up. She's just so *on*. Of course, if his sisters advised him not to jump off a cliff, Tyler would absolutely have to. No way the Mom Police could blame *that* one on us. Mom polices us girls pretty strictly but goes easy on Tyler. Go figure.

Sam loves it when we're all stuck in tents, and the showers are faulty so everyone's pits are über-rank by the third day. She also loves having no summer school and no physio. Doesn't matter that her wheelchair isn't made for those hikes. Tyler just folds her chair into the trunk, whips her over his shoulder, and off we go. I'll say this for Tyler: he's a jerk-face to me, but he's the best big brother to Sammie. And during those camping trips he even reins in the shite he dumps on me most of the time. Maybe because none of his jock friends huddle around as audience.

Either way, for a few long weekends a year, our family sort of works. Mom and Dad take turns driving, and Tyler and Sam and I play backgammon and Schmier and Go Fish in the back. The radio's on, and nobody has to make announcements about their day. Both my parents work, but only my mom has a strict dress code (she's a secretary at an insurance film), so I think one of the reasons she loves vacations is she gets to slob around in jeans and a sweatshirt. And when Mom hits the hay early, Dad lets us slurp tiny sips of rosé wine and mash burnt marshmallows in our mouths till we crash.

The parents pre-book the campgrounds, which are way cheaper than motels. And there's usually a lake to swim in, free of charge. Can't get any more frugal than that and still call it a vacation.

"*This* is what you should do for the summer," Sammie suddenly announced way back before summer, tapping her finger on the map, right at Lake Louise.

"Huh? Whaz you on?" Sammie and I slip into short-hand occasionally. Drives Mom bonkers; she thinks I'm babying Sam.

"Huh yourself. Be a ranger. One of those people who helps us at the campgrounds." She stuck her finger up her nose and then pulled it out, as if to flick something on me.

"Ga-ross," I flicked back. "Thanks for the idea, but I think you have to go to school for, like, a bazillion years before they let you be a Forest Ranger." I wiped my finger along her back, like I had a goober there and just had to leech it onto her.

Sammie isn't exactly good at letting go. Sometimes she wants to play the same game over and over and over or talk about an episode of a show again and again. It *can* get boring, but if you cotton onto how Sammie talks, you can divert the word-flow, create tributaries in the conversation. It's fun, once you get into it. Mom never gets into it.

"It's what you should do for the summer," she repeated.

"Sam. Sa-aa-am." I slowed down my speech. "How can I make your delicate baby-sister brain com-pre-hend? I'd need to train for a gazillion years. I'm not as talented when it comes to summer activities as I am in the winter escapades."

"You're such a doofus. Last summer when we were in the Kananaskis there were, like, oh, a gazillion teenagers running around with

'Junior Dweeb' nametags on their chests. Don't you remember? Tyler hit on anything with boobs. Like that silky girl near Lake Louise."

I sat up so fast I dumped our maps on the floor, and pens scattered under her bed. "Yes!" I shouted. "You're a genius!"

"Duh." She grabbed the red felt pen with both fists and pulled it along some future route on a map.

Turns out, the website explained, there's a Junior Ranger program for teens who want "to expand your horizons and learn to appreciate the outdoors." I read that as a translation for "get away from parents for the summer, and have an adventure that won't cost a bundle." It didn't pay much, but it included job training. Six weeks total, from mid-July till the Labour Day weekend. I'd get home the night before high school started.

"Sam, you're my hero! Oh, and by the way, don't think I didn't notice that you said *boobs!*"

I knew Sita would kill me, as I'd miss major shopping trips and new-school prepping, but I also knew she'd forgive me. I filled out forms, begged for parental signatures, and had to submit an essay. That sucked. An old English assignment? We'd read *The Old Man and the Sea* in grade nine, and every boy in the class picked it for their final essay. Why? Because it was short. Seriously. I'm not great at school, but those boys shoulda figured out by grade four that short does not mean easy. (And, for those who wish to know, my essay was on Margaret Laurence's ginormous *The Diviners*. I am not a genius, but I think I got my A-minus just for picking the fattest book on our teacher's shelf.)

Thinking of those boys, I took the opposite of a shortcut: I wrote a whole new essay. On skating. And not just that I like it—my grade nine teacher wrote on my final essay that liking a novel isn't the same as analyzing a novel—but I tried to show how spinning on the ice makes me feel: bold and dainty at the same time, confident. A risk-taker, but also someone who plans ahead, gauges both the ice and even how steady my legs are. I wrote about how skating on a rink every single morning was like navigating through my teen years, trying to jump and point and balance all at the same time. I was trying to impress them, to show how I could take one situation and apply it to another, winter sport to summer job. I swear I think I impressed them only because I ended my essay by announcing that figure skating made me feel like "a true Canadian girl"! Yuk, but ... I made it onto the short list.

Then the interview, where I just kept repeating that I loved camping, that my family had camped at every provincial park south of Edmonton, and that helping others was my middle name (seriously, how cheesy is that?). Then I recited the name of every campground in southern Alberta—saved by Sammie's maps! When I got home, Mom took both my hands in hers (hand-hugging), and told me that, no matter what, she was proud of me. Yeah, like if you blow the interview, parental pride is an adequate consolation prize. Dad, in his usual spot on the couch, didn't say anything. He acted miffed that I was so willing to miss family vacation time. "Hey," I told him, "this job will help me grow as a person." So he decided not to stay mad. Cheesy *rules*.

When I got the thumbs up, I took Sam to the park and did fourteen cartwheels around her chair. I was so dizzy, I lay down on the see-saw feet-first while Sammie tried to upend me. She didn't have the arm strength, but eventually I toppled and got the appropriate giggle response. Both my siblings like to torture me, but one of them can actually be happy for my happiness.

But those first two weeks of training were so *dull* I thought I'd have to poke my eyes out, just for some excitement. We spent Monday to Friday, and then Monday to Friday, in a classroom. Here in *Calgary*. We had lessons on fire hazards and fire prevention and general fire safety. For rangers, turns out fire is a big deal. A very big deal. On the plus side, I could still get in some skating every morning, so I missed only four weeks of practice, rather than six. Oh, and we also memorized the names of bugs, in case we got lost in the woods, even though we were supervised every minute of every day. As in: which bugs to roast, should we run out of food. Seriously. "Red, orange, yellow, avoid that fellow. Green, black, or brown, wolf it down." And every night we had *homework*, with a test on the final Friday. If we didn't ace the test, that was the end of our summer.

One day, when I mentioned my essay topic, a girl in the training class asked, "Figure skating, or do you mean skateboarding?" And when I confirmed that, yes, I ice skate on a rink in competitions, she was jerk enough to declare, "Wow, how gay." Hardee-har. When I went to Sita's oldest sister Amila's wedding a year ago, their first cousin waved his hands at all the ornate decorations then shout-whispered into his date's ear—loud enough so that everyone in the dance hall could hear—"Weddings are so gay!" Gay as in "awful," "unbearable," or—my all-time-favourite putdown—"lame." Because the only thing worse than being homosexual is being disabled, apparently.

What I should have said was, "Yeah, well, you're here, so now it really is." Or, "Better gay and happy than you and, well, you." But I didn't.

Anyway, I aced the Junior Ranger test. They took us out along the David Thompson Highway, west of Rocky Mountain House to Nordegg. There were different kids there from towns around the province. I didn't see anyone from the Calgary bunch again until the bus trip home on the last day of summer because we got divvied up among the campgrounds. I didn't know anyone, and nobody knew me. How great is that?!

They stationed two of us kids between two provincial parks to do non-native plant control at Ram Falls and work at expanding the Amerada trail at Crimson Lake. That's how Dianne, our group leader (definitely, definitely more on *her*, later), put it: stationed. Like we really were rangers. I know I'm a dork and that I supposedly signed up for this gig to get away from home, but it turns out I got way turned on by doing something *real*. We couldn't arrest people or anything, but we checked out campgrounds, advised people who wanted to fish on which lakes were best, reassured kids about the leech situation, and found lost dogs. Total blast.

And every Sunday just after eight at night (because, given our clientele, weekends were heavy work days), Dianne held a cook-out for us—veggie hot dogs roasted over a campfire (properly set up and doused at the end of the night), burnt marshmallows, sarsaparilla drinks (which, okay, is just root beer, but sounded exotic in Dianne's Australian accent), and grownup talk between ranger Dianne, ranger Ping, me, and the other junior ranger, Surge (absolutely more on *him*, later).

✳

Thing is, I *know* what I'm doing on the ice. I may not ace what Tyler calls "real" sports, but skating turns on my on-switch. Not for me the loneliness of team work. I'm the opposite of Tyler: not mind-blowingly good at many sports, but good enough at this one thing to win trophies. I mean, what self-respecting kid—who has only a slim hope of ending up on the ultimate podium—would choose to get up at 5:45 every morning to practice her figures or to waltz while wearing blades?

Yep, I'm a sports geek. But it's not like I *brag* about getting into Barbie-slut costumes and leaping into the air with skidoos tied to my ankles. No one in junior high cared. But Sita says that high school is all about reputation—not who you are but who people *think* you are. So I'm a skating dweeb. I compete in both the singles (yes, the "ladies" category) and the ice dancing categories. Ice dancing is not at all like the pairs skating you see on TV, where a buff guy is constantly tossing a thin yet definitely muscular woman high into the air. Nope, ice dancing is the one where a boy and a girl (or, at the city-level competitions, usually two girls) squirm their hips together and dance around the rink in sync. Sweet, eh? Don't get Sita started.

Sita cannot fathom—"not even with a gigantic helping of mind-meld," she has informed me—why I'd dance around with another chick holding onto my ass. "And don't tell me it's your hips, not your ass," she'd cut me off. "There you are, a budding young flower, throwing whatever chance you have of hooking up with a popular guy into the Chinook winds." Sita flips her left hand over when she wants to discard a thought. She does her hand-flip, and my entire skating career (career—ha!) gets tossed away. Sometimes I think Sita's going to be a high school guidance counsellor when she grows up. And sometimes I think that and I'm not even joking.

When I'm skating by myself, I can whip around the hockey rink (make no mistake: judges, organizers, even parents think hockey is more important than figure skating—why else would we only get the ice at hours when most teenage boys never see the light of day?) as fast as stink. I can twirl, I can hop, I can hold onto the bottom of my blade and spin so fast you'd puke just imagining it. I used to puke way back when, till my coach taught me about catching one spot on the boards with my eyes, letting go fast, catching, letting go. Helps your balance, and looks cool, too, like your head and body have separated, but somehow don't detach from each other. Like your body can move *bi*-directionally, get it? (I so crack me up.)

In singles, I get to glide and spin and jump and crash down onto the back outside edge of one blade and pull off a tremendous landing. My hair feels like ten million arrows all pointing up, and my shoulders feel like they're scraping the sky. I get to be amazing at all the rough, dangerous, impossible jumps and spins, but I love ice dancing too. So two mornings a week, I also practice skating in perfect alignment with my partner. The skating world is all-inclusive and all that gab, but when the winter Olympics played in Vancouver, a sports station joked that one of the male skaters should get a gender test and maybe compete in the women's competition. Hardee-har. Yep, there are gay and even transgender skaters, but just like other athletes, most stay in the chilled closet till they no longer compete. Also, who'd want to partner up with me if they believed I did the dance routines just to feel them up?

There are usually three couples (sorry: *pairs*) practicing at that point. It's not a problem sharing the rink because ice dancing isn't as rigorous. We go through the routine, we adjust to each other's bodies, we add a turn, we delete a glide.

Around seven a.m., Winnie comes back from her coffee run, and the ~~couples~~ pairs split up into singles. Individually, we get a small portion of the rink to practice our routines and ten minutes each with the entire space. As the competitions loom, each of us will get the full arena for half an hour. Or we can get up at 4:30, convince a community adult to supervise (who must then also get up at 4:30 to make it to the rink by 5:30), and have the whole place to ourselves for an hour. I'm dedicated, but not that dedicated. And *no* mother is that dedicated, not unless the Olympics are involved.

LESBO ALERT: *SHE EXPERIENCES A HEADY PLEASURE FROM WALTZING ON SKATES—WITH GIRLS.*

HET-GIRL ALERT: *SHE NEVER SKATES IN "THE BOY" POSITION DURING WALTZES. SHE'S ALWAYS "THE GIRL."*

CHAPTER FOUR

I miss kissing Surge. When I think about him, I think about how his lips tasted—sweet tea and vanilla. For all I know, his lips were a different flavour every day, but I never had a chance to find out. We only had that one evening and one morning.

We'd stayed up for most of that last night. Dianne and Ping were cool about it as long as we didn't head over to each other's dorm area. We sat by the dwindling campfire and necked and necked and necked.

"Where have you been all my summer?" Surge asked in an excellent movie voice, purring his lips against my neck.

I couldn't tell him I'd been living in Fantasy-Girl land, with Dianne as my protagonist (huh, why wasn't I the protagonist, with Dianne my supporting best?). I shivered at his touch and held onto his upper arms, which were not nearly as scrawny as they looked.

"Yeah, where's the summer when we need it?" How could this be the last day? I'd never kissed anyone before, and I wanted to keep doing it. All night, all night.

The sun set, and Dianne let us stay out by the campfire until she brought me back to the girls' dorm before she herself turned in. While I didn't sleep, the sky changed from golden to pink to crimson to black cherry. Dianne woke me up—musta been a few minutes later. Breakfast and then packing. Summer movie fades to nothing.

At the very end of the very last minute of the very last day, Surge and I exchanged numbers. I told him about the no phone calls rule.

He nodded, like zigzagging around parental restrictions was an obvious obstacle course. Two more kisses during the cellphone conversation. Then a really long hug and more kissing without breaking out of the hug. Ping separated us with the hockey stick they use to prop open the warden's door on sweltering days.

And then the two of us got on two separate buses, one going north, one south. But I found seven texts from him when I pulled out my phone just past Red Deer. And in addition to the texts, he'd left two voice mail messages by the time my bus reached Airdrie. The sunburned fields rolled by as our van zoomed down Highway 2. I texted him back; I thanked him for leaving his voice. I apologized again that we couldn't talk live. Not even voicemail, I reminded him. And I promised him words waiting on his pillow when he woke up. Total: five texts. Was I ever loving this whole slushy-gushy phase!

The next day, my first day at J.J. Backstrom High, he left three more texts, each one with fewer exclamation points:

"i miss u ! ! ! !"

"i miss u ! !"

"miss u."

In the past, Sita drilled it into me not to come off as too eager, but boy, was I eager! Once school started, I'd send him a text in the morning, usually while waiting for the adult supervisor to unlock the rink at 6:29 a.m., and then again just before bed. Surge texted me at odd times during the day, and even left a phone message though I'd reminded him to text only.

"u deep in 1st wk? im kul w/ skul."

Or: "c wat sum gud kssg leeds 2?"

Or: "i b misng u."

Don't judge; my messages back aren't any more academically brilliant than Surge's shorthand. I have a secret lover, a *great-kissing* secret lover.

❋

I definitely can't talk to my parents, and I'm apparently too much of a jellyfish to broach the bisexual subject with Sita. I mean, I haven't even told her about Surge yet. Truth be true, I've barely broached the subject with *myself*. To help, I decide to google "lesbian/straight/bi/ confused/horny" and see what the internet gods recommend. Problem is, we only have one computer. For the entire family! And the Mom Police keeps it in the dining room where absolutely everyone can see the screen from the kitchen. Trust issues much?!

Plus, Tyler probably knows how to trace my browser sites, even if I erased my web history. And Tyler would *not* be understanding or kind about any secret I'd try to keep. Same story with the computer labs at school. They're almost never free, and even when they are, someone's bound to walk in just as my careful search produces an explicit dyke porn site. Yikes.

So when Sita's in Drama Club (yeah, and *I'm* the dork?), I head for the public library. No one I know goes there. I have to pay to update my library card, but then I can use whatever computer I want. And it helps. Sort of.

I get a list of about nine billion sites and check out the first fourteen. Sites like "How To Find Your Inner Lesbian," "Bi in Denial," and "Straight Girls who Love Lesbian Porn." A lot of kids write to various sites confessing that they're "bi-curious." Which means I'm not alone. Nice to know, but doesn't help me figure things out. "You're lying to yourself," too many of them tell me. But, "Don't put a label on yourself," is another piece of advice. That doesn't help at all, just makes me long more for a label in giant neon floodlights. I walk home from the library as diminished as the fading light outside. Who do you talk to when you can't even figure the questions out? Maybe Friday, with Sita ...

✳

Seven hundred kids in this new high school. Last year, Sita and I decided to get all sophisticated as part of the graduating class of junior high. We'd spend afternoons slurping double mochaccinos, window shopping, and talking about who we'd kiss on the rugby team. Yup, that's our social life in a nutshell: sugar and boys.

This year, though, we'll only have Friday afternoons. I'll be at different dentists' offices Tuesdays and Thursdays. And Sita's Drama Club meets Mondays and Wednesdays right after school. So every Friday after last bell, we plan to meet at Sita's locker and swing out toward the second-closest coffee shop. The closest café doesn't provide enough of a post-school buffer—too many teachers will head there if they have a sport to coach or an activities club to sponsor or if they're in charge of Detention that day. On Fridays, Mr Grier is the regular jailer. He seems mostly okay, except for a bad case of high expectations, but who wants to run into *any* teacher outside of school?

Meanwhile: the joy of Frosh Week. Despite having an older brother who goes to J. J. Backstrom, Tyler never plays big brother, except to torment me. In fact, if I run into him in the halls this first week, I will totally have to suffer through an old-fashioned froshing, like being pelted with condoms filled with ketchup and mayo. Although one of my brother's goons will probably do his dirty work. Thank the Sibling Gods I have Sam.

The way normal people do it, kids come along every couple of years, right? Speaking of "normal," and how my parents *aren't*, take Sam. Not literally, I like her just where she is, thanks! (Oh, I crack me up!) She's eight years younger than me, ten years younger than Tyler. And since my parents were so eager to get married and have kids and join the grownup workforce when they were in their teens, I'm pretty sure Tyler and I are part of the package they pre-ordered without reading the fine print. Sam, on the other hand, was probably a birth-control accident. In an age when every kid out there knows how to use a condom, my parents managed to get knocked-up long after they thought they'd finished having kids.

Which means they were fornicating in their forties. Okay, okay, Sam's seven, which means that the parents had only reached their late thirties when they conceived her, but I'm a sucker for alliteration. I'm addicted to the almighty alliterative axiom. I'm revved up for the repeats. Or as Mr Grier, my English Lit teacher. says, I'm no good at "real" poetry (sucky quotation marks his and, yes, he makes finger curls as he speaks) so I make do with pathetic word tricks rather than doing the work of coming up with a strong image. Or a convincing word.

"You are addicted to alliterative *phrases*," he corrects me. It's only my second English class of the year, and the teacher's already on my back. "Axiom is not the word you're looking for, but like all lazy poets, you choose the word for its convenience, rather than for where it can take you in the next line."

Yes, he really talks like that. In junior high, my language arts teachers divided up the semester so that we spent an entire unit on grammar, a unit on the short story, a unit on the novel, one on Canadian literature, half a unit on the persuasive essay, and the other half on the analytical essay, and then we somehow ran out of time when it was supposed to be the poetry unit, three days before the final exam.

Not Mr Grier. He's such a hard-ass that he thinks we should all be able to write essays that might get published some day. Published! Like who besides a die-hard teacher cares what high school students think about Romeo falling in love with the wrong rich girl? The course syllabus shows the entire first month taken up with poets. By the end of next week, we're to have covered bpNichol, dionne brand, and Gwendolyn MacEwen. Separate assignments and a quiz for each one. After that, he has two Shakespeare plays planned, four novels, and then he wants to return to poetry!

On the very last day of class, we'll each have to recite a poem—"with succinct analysis"—in front of the entire class. And not just any poem, but one we write ourselves. No rhymes, unless you want a big fat F. And no alliteration.

"That last rule's just for Keira," Grier adds.

So, if anyone else in the class wants to pair "almighty" with "axiom," it's apparently A-okay with Mr Grier.

On Wednesday, I get lost between Period Two and Period Three. I can*not* find my next class to save my life. I dash out as soon as the Period Two bell rings and search every hallway for my next class. There are hordes of kids banging lockers and tripping younger kids and racing off to smoke during a free period. All the hallways look the same, and the numbering system makes no sense. In defeat, I finally head to the front office. And this secretary who helps me is so nice that I feel worse than humiliated. Turns out, I have back-to-back math classes in the same room. I think about claiming cramps and asking to go to the nurse's office, but with my luck: A) Somehow a bulletin will go out that I'm on the rag, and B) I won't be able to find the nurse's office. When I finally (fifteen mins late!) make my way *back* to my math class, Ms Temmie doesn't even look up. I guess she figured I needed a bathroom break between sessions.

The thing is, between my skating and part-time work and Sita's parents actually expecting her to not only pass but achieve excellent grades, we won't get much time to hang out together. Hence the absolute need for a coinciding lunch schedule. J.J. Backstrom High is so big that there are two rotations for lunch. Which sounds reasonable, but absolutely isn't. For one thing, a lot of the clubs meet over the lunch hour, and with this schedule, kids either can't meet all at the same time, or they have to choose a club based not on their interests but on what time they eat their club sandwich. (Get it? I really crack me up!) So, yeah, I feel for the yearbook kids. I may not be into photography and making every freaking school moment a *memento mori* (google it), but if I had to choose between eating and skating, my life would be a mess. Truly. My body needs constant feeding in order to have the energy to power-skate through sleep time.

When Sita has lunch, I'm in Biology. The only other grade ten Biology class takes place late on Thursdays when I have to boot it to the city bus. Dentists' offices close early, and the Thursday job doesn't come with a key. The dental hygienist stays till 3:35 to let me in, and the door locks behind me. By 3:40, she's out of there. I don't blame her (*he* never stays an extra five minutes), but I have to have a free period last class that day, just for the privilege of cleaning crusted spit off miniature sinks.

Without Sita, I end up having lunch with Amanda Forsythe, Joline Tamineau, and Joline's two minions. Amanda, who loves all shades of green and today wears a loose shamrock T over lime shorts, has always been nice to me. Maybe she's grateful. In grade two, she peed her pants and when I saw, I raised my hand to go to the bathroom, then slipped her wads and wads of toilet paper upon my return. Amanda and I play nice when we have time, but my schedule is chock-full, and she's usually trying to hang out at the jock table or the goth table or the chess-players table, or ... you get the picture. We're friends, but not each other's main lifeline.

Joline and I have known each other for years and years and years, but not really as friends, not since a long time ago. We know each other because our moms know each other. They used to be incredibly close friends, and so we hung around in our underpants back when friendship wasn't a choice as much as a parental accessory. But even when our mothers stopped visiting regularly, they still expected us to be friends. Parents are ridic that way. Just because you're around the same age, you should hang out together? Is this how it works for them? Is this how it's *ever* worked for anyone older than about four?

Once, when I was seven and Joline Tamineau was six, we stuck our tongues together and tried to walk around without letting them untouch. Perhaps some tame version of playing doctor. (Come to think of it, we *did* start out with tongue depressors in the sandbox.)

Our backyard is the size of a balcony porch, a landing strip for a toy airplane. So when Joline and I crab-walked, tongues attached, around the yard, we hit the fence, tripped over the pots that held my dad's tomatoes, and fell into the sandbox—our tongues cemented together with saliva. Tyler swooped in on his bicycle and didn't even wait for the image to register before he burned right out again, his tires grumbling over the gravel. No big deal. Tyler—when he wasn't hiding my shoes or stuffing my pillow case with licorice jelly beans (yes, I'm allergic to black licorice. Not get-to-the-hospital-or-die allergic, just bad asthma and eczema break-out allergic)—was pretty good at plain old ignoring me.

No, wait: that's wrong.

"Only fags like to lick other fags," he snarled at us as he rode his bike around from the frontyard to the back, trying to balance on his knees on the banana seat, and not letting me get past. "Joe-ly and Key-rah sitting in a tree," he said as his bike pedal swiped my calf, "k-i-s-s-i-n-g!"

Joline slapped his banana seat, and his bike teetered. He kicked me as he rode past us, then zoomed out of the yard.

"You two are sick!" he yelled back. "Diseased! Lezzie-infected!"

Being a fag didn't sound like a good thing, so Joline and I unstuck our tongues and played sandbox until her mother scooped her up to go.

Not long after that, our mothers stopped visiting with each other. So Joline and I stopped visiting with each other, too. And Tyler caught me supergluing pink football stickers onto his helmet and a whole new temper frenzy ensued.

Since then, Joline has been a bit of a thorn in my kidney region. She tripped me in a mall once, and called me "Key-her-in-the-ear-a!" in a movie theatre one time.

This cafeteria consists of rows of long tables shoved together, short edge to short edge, with kids cramming to sit in clumps with their friends. The special on Tuesdays is mushy spaghetti, and no grade ten student with any sense would order that dish, first week of school. Apparently, being a slob in grade eleven is totally acceptable. All around me, I smell garlic and butter on the cusp of being rancid, and underneath that, heavy fumes of deep-fried sugar. Mom makes me pack a home-made lunch, which today I'm grateful for. I choose a dessert in the bustling Backstrom buffet (okay, okay, Mr Grier, I get it) and sit with Amanda when Joline Tamineau and her two robot girls walk up to our mostly empty table. Joline somehow looks exactly like she did when she was eight, but way, way tougher.

When I see Joline, I assume it's to steal a doughnut off my plate. But her mother must have said something because here she is politely loitering at my table. Joline is being so courteous, I'm getting worried. She does slap my arm, but I think it's supposed to be friendly.

"Make room, losers," Joline barks out. I'm kinda relieved, in a weird way.

"Joline, this is Amanda."

"Hey. These are The Two." Joline plonks herself down at the table with us, and the robots follow her every move. I can't tell if this is a nickname they figured was way-suave years ago and are now stuck with or if they hate it, but Joline calls the shots. I discover, as she scarfs down a tofu wrap that one of the robots dutifully hands to her, that Joline skipped grade seven: her teachers bumped her from elementary school to the middle of junior high, and she's hung out with The Two ever since. Why don't they just call each other The Three, then? Where's Sita when you need a really snippy comment?

Oh, right, Sita has Language Arts during my lunch period. But not *any* Language Arts class. She has Mr Munson, whose students read one Shakespeare (because, really, you can't escape *Macbeth* in a grade ten lit class) and one existentialist novel a year (usually Camus' *The Outsider*, probably because it's short), and that's it. By the end of the second day, every grade ten kid already knows the back-story gossip on Munson.

He was originally a Spanish teacher, but the school board cut all second languages except French about a decade ago. Munson got shuffled over to English Lit because, apparently, language is language, right? And right around the same time as the shuffle, he got engaged to the principal, who dumped him before the year was up and then transferred herself to another high school. So he was stuck with a class he didn't sign up to teach and an existential heart. Grim, right? Yeah, except everybody knows, even us newbies, that Munson doesn't care about Shakespeare at all and gives absolutely anyone a B-plus if they don't make trouble and hand in an essay detailing the bleakness of regular existence. A boring class but an easy one.

So by the third day of lunch period, I'm getting used to eating lunch without Sita. I pass Joline the salt when she asks for it and watch grimly as she proceeds to salt everyone's fries, not just her own. I'd harrumph, but who else can I eat lunch with?

"So, I switched to Language Arts with Grier," Sita announces as she plunks down at our table during lunch period, *my* lunch period. It's the mid-lunch frenzy. The din has reached World Cup sudden-death overtime level. What?! No way Sita voluntarily switched to a harder English Lit class just to hang out. Just to hang out with *me*.

"Scoot over," she demands, because apparently even my ass doesn't believe Sita is really here. Amanda scoots over, not looking as thrilled as I feel. Guess she doesn't love third place on the friendship wheel. I'll have to think about that. Later.

As my ass recovers, so does my mouth: "Woo hoo!" I shout. "What? How? With Grier?"

Sita just shrugs. "I read anyway. May as well be for homework."

And that's that. We magically gain an extra hour, Monday to Friday. And while Amanda may be angling for lunchtimes with just her and me, I don't feel especially shitty, because I remember from junior high that whenever Amanda gets around to seeing a boy, I eat alone.

No one wants to eat alone. And it's not that I have no other friends, but, well, with skating every free minute, plus working after school ... I don't exactly have a lot of friends. And no matter what boy Sita slobbers over during Calculus, she never abandons me to eat with him—unless *he* eats with *us*. Sita would never join the guy at *his* table. Unless my being *not*-just-boy-crazy scares her away, my best friend would never abandon me.

LESBO ALERT: *SHE PREFERS LUNCH WITH GIRLS, SIPPING LATTES WITH GIRLS, TALKING/CHATTING/GABBING WITH GIRLS.*

HET-GIRL ALERT: *SHE'D RATHER EAT LUNCH WITH A GIRL SHE DOESN'T MUCH LIKE THAN SIT BY HERSELF IN A MEATBALL MALODOROUS CAFETERIA.*

CHAPTER FIVE

So, high school problem number one: solved. For this entire semester, Sita and I share lunch period. And Social Studies (though we don't get to sit anywhere near each other, thanks to Rumpled, I mean Mr Rempel). And English Lit thrice weekly (are you impressed, Mr Grier? I used an old-timey British word). Mornings, we walk to school together, then we have fifty-five minutes during lunch to catch up on the morning scandals and a wave or two in the afternoons as we each rush by toward Math or Chemistry or Gym. And Friday afternoons.

Which means, really, that I don't have any excuse to keep avoiding "the conversation," the "what I did on my summer vacation" chat. The "bi" chat. Sita will be thrilled to hear about Surge, right? But then there's my crush on Dianne, who spent days pointing out hazelnut bushes and Saskatoon berries to us. I don't want to damage my friendship with Sita, but I also can't tell her only part of this story. It would mean telling her about only part of myself, and I need Sita to embrace all of me. (Not literally, of course. What do you think I am, a *homo*?)

We also have Saturday nights, if Sita can sweet-talk her parents into letting her party with me. That's how she puts it to them, that the two of us deserve to "party" together. And she doesn't do the hand-wave when she talks to her parents. "We'll hang out at the mall, stay at the coffee shop till closing, no adults, no other kids." And I need to make sure to get her home by ten. "For goddess' sake, it's not like we ever give our parents epic trouble," Sita points out. As long as her homework is done, her parents are A-okay with us going out on Saturday nights. Sita actually says, "A-okay."

My parents have the same rule, but only in principle. It's a given that my homework has to be done and gone over by the Mom Police and pressed into perfect sandwich bags before Sunday. Sunday is for chores and skating and one dentist's office and a family meal as final punctuation. So if I haven't gotten my homework done and done *well* by late Saturday afternoon, it's unlikely it will get done at all. One week into school, and they're already unhappy about Sita and me "hanging" at the mall every Saturday night.

"We don't hang at the mall," I explain, as I'm helping Mom cut up carrots for an after-school snack (good thing I had doughnuts again for lunch). "Well, we might, or we might walk over to the skateboard park, or just sit around her basement watching *Angel* reruns" (vampire with a soul—cracks me up!).

"Even when I was a teenager, walking around stores never seemed a very satisfying weekend activity." My mother. She's unloading groceries, piling stuff for supper on one counter and a midnight meal for Dad when he's at work on another.

I'm getting good at dodging her flying sentences, but then my dad joins in. "Isn't the skateboard park where all the drug deals go down?" Dad usually lets me alone, though he doesn't trust the world he lives in once the sun sets. Still, he leaves the rules and regulations mostly to Mom. But when he does come down hard about homework or tidying our rooms, we all scurry.

Once, when Dad was giving me driving lessons, he told me

all about T-intersections, how people think drivers going straight ahead on the T have the right of way, but they don't. "So," he lectured, "if the intersection has no stop sign, then whichever driver is on the right has the right-of-way. Same as a regular intersection. Got it?" I nodded.

"Ha! You may have the right of way, but being right doesn't do you much good if you're crushed under a two-ton. Always stop. Always proceed cautiously." I nodded again. He's right (that's what they taught us in Drivers Ed, too), but he's only right about here because whenever we drive down to Montana, the rules change. With Dad, you just have to go along, which is easier than an unending argument. He just doesn't adjust. As long as I play the devoted daughter and let Dad be bossy about things that don't matter, we get along fine.

My parents are waaaaay more suspicious than Sita's about where we go and how long we'll go for. As long as she's with me, Sita's parents give us a trusting leash. The hilarious thing is that my mother thinks Sita is a good influence on me. We should swap mothers. They'd be happier with their daughters, and we'd get so much less hassle. I duck behind the couch as if to pick up some playing cards that dropped there, but really I text Sita that the parents are getting to me: "PLS trade? my mom luvs u!"

When Mom let me work one afternoon a week in junior high, the very first purchase I made was phone minutes. Sita had an extra cell from her cousin who visited and just left it behind when he flew back to Vancouver. He pretended to lose it because he wanted an upgrade. It works fine, and here's the genius of my teen buying power: I never use the phone as a phone. *Never*.

Mom would've flipped if I'd "waltzed in" with a cellphone after my first paycheque. Instead, I "inherited" the phone from Sita, bought into a plan that had few call minutes and lengthy texting, and I was set. Though I did almost use up all my texting in the first week. Seriously. Nowadays, I can pump out two or three texts in about seven seconds flat. I got that phone just in time, cuz being gone all August, I needed to be able to text with Sita.

Tyler has plans for a big kegger this weekend, and the parental units will let him go, no question. Because he's older? Or because he's a boy? Tyler has a one a.m. curfew on Saturdays. Not only do I have to be back by ten, but my parents have a special no-bend-statute that says if I arrive even one minute past the hour (kitchen clock rules), my curfew goes down by a half hour the next week. And so on.

My parents think they know kids. They think they have a special key that opens the teen-lingo danger-code. They don't trust malls or skateboard parks. They think we're going to sneak off to a party and make out with boys. Truth be true, we're going to sneak off to a party and ... make out with boys. Well, only Sita will do the second part. Sita says we have to stop being the goody-good girls (like that's our nickname or something) and crash a few parties.

"What do you mean by 'crash'?" I ask her, sounding suspiciously like my suspicious parents. It's Friday—the end of our first week at Backstrom. We've survived Frosh Week. We decide to walk and walk and walk. A good time to start my confession? As soon as I think this, my neck gets hot and my feet feel clunky. If I tell Sita, will she expect me to cruise girls at this party? I nearly trip as we head down a steep hill towards the Bow River. For now, I keep my tongue safely stored behind my teeth.

"Find out where the weekend parties are, pick the best one, and show up." She does the little hand-wave. "Easy-peasy." Sita has a squadron of older sisters who actually talk to her, so she knows all about parties and older boys and which teachers to avoid at Backstrom. Or at least thinks she does. We've reached the river and follow it downtown.

"That part, yes," I concede. "Very easy to follow the gossip trail to find out about the party, *but*." But we're still not invited. But our parents still won't let us go.

"They don't check your invitations at the door, Ms Watches Too Much TV from the Last Century." The hand-wave again. Sita heads for the bicycle path that snakes its way beside the river, running from one end of town to the other. She ignores the angry grunts from serious cyclists who don't want to slow down for meanderers. "Yeah, yeah, I know, the nineties really crack you up, but this is *now*. You just show up at the door and, *voil*à, party."

That's not my point. "Okay, yeah, um, I was thinking more about how we'd get *out*." I wait for the sarcasm.

"Oh, right." Another hand-wave. "That's exactly what we need our invitations for—the huge bouncers who won't let you leave." She makes this announcement at the ginormous wooden staircase. We've reached the bottom of the Crescent Heights cliff. From the top there's a spectacular view of downtown and the river and even the mountains, way to the west. But first you have to climb about a billion steps. We climb with our backs to the view, counting steps as we march up and up and up.

"Look, I *know* it's not about invitations." What kind of a double-dork does she think I am? I may not be a make-out expert, but I'm not hopeless. "But you and I don't just have to get into the party, we have to *leave* the party when, let's face it, the party is probably just getting started." I underline the point: "We make all the effort of busting into one of the cool-kid parties, and then leave before ten? Forget being known as goody-goods, we'll be Cinderellas. Or worse" (trust me, there's *always* a worse nickname to be had), "because at least Cinderella got to stay out till the witching hour."

We plunk down on a wooden landing half-way up, where the stairs zigzag, wrapping our legs around the wooden poles, chins resting on the bottom rung of the handrails, pretending we're enamoured with the view and we just have to stop and gaze, right that minute. People jog these steps every day, up and down, more than once. If I hadn't just taken a month off my daily skating practice, would I be able to run up and down these steep steps, too? I start sweating just thinking about what Winnie will say if I don't qualify in the Regionals. Winnie dreams about Olympic rings and podiums, but am I up for all that?

"Hmm." Sita finally rejoins the conversation. "Okay, I'll think of something."

The thing about letting a straight-A student come up with solutions is that she'll do it, no matter how drastic. We unwrap chocolate bars and munch away, the entire downtown at our feet. In less than ten minutes, Sita comes up with the *perfect* plan for us to get to a party by 8:50, hang out with cool kids from our school (and quite a few older kids not from our school), and get out by 9:47.

"It's about time you kissed a boy anyway," Sita says.

"Says you." I have *got* to tell her about Surge, but—

"You'll be lucky if you actually like kissing your boyfriend. Forget about liking your first kiss ever."

Instead of correcting her, I pull my legs in so I don't trip joggers crazy enough to run *up* these stairs. "Don't you even *like* kissing?"

"Of course I like kissing," she answers. "But the first kiss with most guys is usually slobbering and too quick and you're too nervous and he's, well, he doesn't care as much as you do. Way better to get it over with, with someone you don't even have the hots for."

"Okay, okay. But the deal's off for this party if Tyler's there." And that is exactly the right thing to say to convince Sita that I'm in. Her plan is for us to go, scope things out for a while, and then let two random boys drag us outside for a make-out session. That way, we get to the party, we get seen at the party, and then everyone assumes we spend the rest of the party making out—not leaving because of a ridiculously early and uncool curfew. I have to admit, the plan has no flaws. Except for *me*, of course.

Look, I'm a girl who wants to proclaim her bisexuality yet is terrified of a random make-out session. Terrified to spend an evening kissing a boy I don't even know, terrified to tell Sita that I maybe wouldn't mind if I were kissing a girl. As far as my best friend *4evAH* is concerned, no one's even tried to kiss me.

In grade nine there were a lot more boys that I wanted to kiss than there are now in grade ten. Either boys are getting less adorable as they age or I'm getting closer and closer to the other end of bisexuality. Or maybe I'm just feeling loyalty to my summer fling? ("Fling" is an exaggeration, for sure. Still, I am not as inexperienced as Sita thinks.)

I get up to climb the rest of the stairs. I'm just too panicked to sit still. "But aren't we still in the same pickle with your plan?" I demand. "How do we get out of jail free, once it's time to go?"

Sita explains that she has her eyes on three guys she knows will be at this particular party. So as we walk up to the top of the crescent, she explains how the amended plan will go: She flirts with one or all of them, and when it's time to go outside, I tag along. I'm the best friend too sad to get her own date. She makes out a bit with Boy Number Lucky (Sita's nickname) and then I drag her off, cuz we're supposed to be at this party together. Boy Number Lucky goes back inside, and we slip out the garden gate. We get home by 9:59. My parents are impressed by my ability to make curfew, Sita's by sticking to her agreement to hang out with Keira only.

And that is pretty much how we manage our first high school party that weekend.

Crowded hallways in the house and beer cans everywhere on the front lawn, a keg surrounded by ice in the bathtub, and kids chugging as a way to celebrate successfully getting through the first week of school. Except for the excitement of getting in, I don't really get off being there. Too many kids squash into the kitchen and living room for me to join their conversations. Downstairs in the family room, so many couples—straight couples—are making out, I feel like I'm in a porn flick, and I head back up the stairs pretty quickly. When I go to sit on the living room floor, a grade eleven girl squishes over so I can perch on the arm-rest of the couch. I think she's making room to be friendly, but she's macking on the boy next to her.

All this public action makes me long for Surge's lips. When he kissed me, only the birds and the bees (and a couple of otters) hung around as witnesses. How corny is that? Most of August, Surge and I spent hours together talking about the disappearing grizzlies, our favourite hike in an area that was due to be clear-cut by next summer, or how we'd divvy up the next day's chores. Okay, arguing about how we'd divvy up the next day's chores.

Turns out, his parents signed him up to be a junior ranger without even asking him, submitting one of his school essays for the application. When the interview rolled around, Surge wasn't even sure what he was interviewing *for*.

"Hey, I thought it would at least be a high-paying job." Surge laughed as he zinged a flat stone into the middle of an abandoned beaver pond. "Man, if the guy conducting that interview had asked me why I wanted a training position, I'd've been out of there like lightning. I was *so* pissed at my parents, but I went, cuz by that point I really had to get away from them!"

"Yeah, I did it for the parental escape route, too," I admitted.

"You?" he asked, like he figured me for some kind of home-body.

"It's a total trip to be out in the wilderness without relatives," I told him. And at that point I actually wondered if I should ask him about my longing to kiss Dianne. Surge thought she was a bit stuck-up, but he must have thought she was okay to look at; I caught him staring at her a couple of times. Sure, I figured, he might freak about me being a homo, but that day was our last day of summer. He blasted a pine cone against a tree. Surge was hard to read. On the one hand, he seemed too cool to be cool, you know? On the other, he was from Bonnyville, and staying a week in Edmonton for training (the kids from the boonies got everything condensed into seven solid days) was the most time he'd ever spent in a big city.

"We do a fair bit of camping in my family," I told him. "I had to get away, but no way my parents would agree to let me wander around, say, Vancouver for a month." I didn't admit to Surge that they couldn't afford to let me spend a summer anywhere else, either. "But I'm glad I had this summer, and not just because I got to get away from my family," I added. The sky looked bluer than I'd ever seen, and the black spruce branches cut across that blue. "Actually, it's been a fabuloso month." I breathed in pine needles and wild roses and the end of summer.

Dianne had sent Surge and me to check campsites for properly doused fire pits, and to collect bits of garbage that people think it's all right to leave behind for the magic elves to clean up. He chucked another stone over the pond. I thought maybe he still wished he'd spent the last four weeks working at the Co-op grocery store with his buddies. I tried to figure out what he was thinking from his expression, but all I saw were his eyes squinting up against the blaze of the afternoon sun. Before we kissed, I noticed his pale green eyes a lot more than his succulent lips.

My Surge daydream dumps me back at the crowded party when

I hear Sita meeting up with the first Boy Number Lucky (Tony). But after chatting with him for zero-point-eight seconds, she gives him the hand-flick (same as the hand-wave, but with more contempt) and moves into the kitchen to grab a beer. The living room, with a bay window that's wide open, has clumps of kids passing joints and nodding to the Chainsmokers tune blaring from a laptop shoved sideways onto a bookshelf. Mostly, the boys lean back against the walls with their eyes closed. The music blares, and a grade ten girl I vaguely recognize passes around a guitar-shaped bong. I'm still holding my first beer and thinking about pouring its contents into the droopy ficus tree next to the couch, but I just keep warming the can in my hands. I don't totally love the taste of beer, and I'm not about to down anything stronger, not with my first fall skating session with Winnie tomorrow afternoon.

From where I sit, I can watch the living room crowd, see into the kitchen, and observe who's still coming in the front door. When I spot Sita with Daz, the second Boy Number Lucky, I can tell she likes him more than the other boys—no hand-wave for him. But he's in grade eleven, and we've already learned that most boys don't want to hang out with what they consider immature newbies. Nothing immature about Sita. She perches on the kitchen counter and leans into his laugh as he tells her stories with his hands and arms and his entire body. Definitely a theatre guy. At 9:41, she hops off the counter and walks out the back door, so I get up to follow.

This is where it gets a bit sticky. I mean, am I supposed to sit beside them while they go at each other? By now, I should trust Sita. We get outside, and she introduces Daz to me. "My friend and

I are heading out," she says. "But I'll see you in Drama Club, right?" And then she leans up and kisses him on the chin, soft and sweet. And we deke out the back garden gate.

On the way home, I'm all worried that success at one such party will lead to sneaking around every other weekend. Have I mentioned that I'm a dweeb? And that I have to be up at a *ridic* hour on weekend mornings? "Relax," she tells me, just before we part ways, "I met a guy. You will too."

We spend the next Saturday night at the coffee shop so I can hear all about Daz: "He likes playing the trumpet, but just for fun, he's not in the marching band or anything." Trumpet player implies cool. Marching band, not so much. Then I hear some more: "Daz really likes reality shows, for, like, the irony." They're not officially a couple yet, but Sita's definitely smitten. She goes over and over the details she's already told me: how many minutes they talked on the phone last night (thirty-seven); how tall he is (the perfect amount taller than she is for kissing); how he smells like ginger ale and winter coats.

And I don't mind listening. We curl into a corner at the coffee shop, slurping mochaccinos and batting words back and forth, just like we used to slam tetherballs over and over in grade one. The last thing I want is to gross Sita out. I pull my drink closer and lean down to slurp the whip-cream topping. *I'm a coward*, I think to myself. I have to tell Sita that—just maybe—the reason I'm not kissing boys at a party is cuz I'm holding out for something else. Am I holding out for Surge? Am I holding out for some fictional girl? I don't know. I have *such* a story for my best friend, but once

I start, I'll have to tell her the whole story. I'll have to expose *me*.

HET-GIRL ALERT: *SHE PUTS GLITTER ON HER FACE FOR A PARTY, EVEN THOUGH THAT IS SO 2012.*

LESBO ALERT: *SHE REFUSES TO SULLY HERSELF BY KISSING BOYS SHE DOESN'T KNOW.*

CHAPTER SIX

That night, after making it to her house by quarter after nine (the coffee shop closes at nine anyway), I go in with Sita, just like I'm an old-timey gentleman after a chaste date, and we gab in her bedroom for nearly an hour. Sita's locker at school screams "neat freak," but her bedroom is a freakin' mess. Just like all her sisters before her (all but one has moved out), she throws clothes on the floor (yes, clothes that she will wear again and yet manage to look neat as a pin supposedly looks), stuffs books under the duvet, and drops change on any surface that doesn't tilt. Don't even get me started on the rubber snakes and felt lizards peeking out from underneath her bed and piled high in her closet. Sita collects all things reptile, so herds of stuffed and plastic creatures crowd her bookshelves and bed and even the windowsill. No way my parents would allow such a "creative" display in our bedrooms. "Put it away, or I take it away," the Mom Police threatens. Luckily, she's too busy with work and dinner and Sammie's extra-curricular to follow through on all her threats. In a gesture of duty, Tyler's been folding his T-shirt collection.

So Sita and I play scrunched-paper basketball using a crumpled chip bag as the basket and repeat every rude remark Max Bledsoe got away with this week. But at 9:56, I grab my coat, shove my boots on without lacing them, and run home. In bed, I go over the conversation we didn't have, the one that starts, "Sita, I have Big News," but then I get distracted thinking about kissing Surge. The first time we kissed, my lips burst from the inside out. The second time we kissed, I could hear the clouds spiral and the leaves drip off the trees. Seriously.

Evil nemesis that my brain is, once I start to think about Surge's body, I also think about Marisol's. We share science and math classes. Her nose scrunches up when she tries to calculate with rational numbers. On Thursday, she passed me a note about her much older sister's *Zombie Marathon* addiction. "Seriously archaic AR! does she know she's 27?!" Marisol wears clothes inherited from that much older yet much less buxom sister. Which means her own curvy "buxom" bursts out at you. At me. At lunch, Marisol sits with Raf and the other gamers. Sadly, my infamous cell phone can't even capture regular photos, let alone A.R. creatures, so Marisol and I don't have much to talk about. I fall asleep transported onto that fallen log on the naturally sandy beach at Crimson Lake, my brain summoning the image of Marisol nuzzling Surge's neck. Hoo boy.

※

The next Tuesday, after I get home from my job at Dr So's office, Mom tells me that I should balance the tension of skating and school and work with yoga—*as if*. Bad enough coming home after school to find your mother in the middle of the house practicing Plow pose (that's when you lie on your back, your arms go where your legs should be, and your legs reach above your head, toes to the floor—totally weirded me out the first time I saw her do this!), but imagine if I'd come home with a friend? Or a date? Mothers and spandex: *not* a good image. No wonder I'm single—it's not my confused hormones, it's my mother. Anyway, these days, Mom's looking a bit puckered around the eyes, so why should I believe that yoga helps her relax?

Tyler pops his head into the kitchen but not enough of his body to get roped into helping with any vegetable chopping or table setting. He's wearing a T-shirt with the slogan, "I hate being the greatest, but it's my job." Yeah, right.

Tyler has done things like rip posters off my walls and belittle my friends (when I'm foolish enough to invite anyone besides Sita over), and he calls me Stickbean when his friends are around. Once Sita asked, "Isn't it *String*bean?" Luckily Tyler didn't hear. Tyler does not do well when people correct him. And don't go thinking that he's a tough-ass who likes to bully his own sister but will step in if anyone else tries to get in her face. Nope. He'll lead potential tormenters right *to* my face. He'll post the road signs.

Have I mentioned that Tyler is a turd? He's a turd. No, he's a jackass. No, wait, he's the turd *from* a jackass. Tyler is almost two years older and seventeen years meaner than me. According to my parents, who cannot entirely be trusted on this one, he was totally infatuated with me when I originally showed up and spent the first year of my life trying to hold me (not easy for a toddler), talking baby-talk to me, and giving me every one of his toys, every chance he had—even as they mysteriously reappeared in his room on a nightly basis. So: total adoration and I can't even bask in the memory of it.

My brother plays sports not because he likes basketball or soccer or—god forbid—football, but because he's good at them, and he likes to be better than anyone else at everything else. For Tyler, soccer is boring and football "too mathematical," but he plays because teachers like a high school kid who exhibits team spirit. And because girls like jocks. Yes, girls like jocks. Most girls. Enough girls. But the same girls who like boy jocks do *not* like girl jocks. Tyler's good at football, despite hating the math part of the game. But one of the things I like about skating is the calculating and planning and measuring of how close you land to the boards, trying to keep the jump at the same height but landing a few millimetres over. I make up all my own Singles routines (with Winnie's final approval) and most of the other girls' Duo Dance routines (yep, very few teenage boys in my figure skating association). The other girls trust me because my routines fit *them*, not the music.

Skaters make three mistakes when choosing a song for their dance routines:

A) Techno-drivel.
B) They want the latest single sensation, and by the time the competition rolls around they end up with an over-played Lady Gaga or Cold Play hit.
C) They let their parents choose the song and end up with, like, Hall & Oates (google it). Except even most of the competition judges aren't *that* old.

In skating, the wrong tune kills your routine. You have to choose music that helps your body open itself to the ice. I know, I know, that's practically yoga-speak, but something magical happens when you pull off just the right spin with just the right high note. Or can kick your leg high enough in the right spot to get you through a rough patch. So I piece together routines that will allow me to whip my skinny, boney body into a frenzy and blast most of the other competitors out of the (frozen solid) water (yeah, yeah, cheesy—but Winnie always says that we should skate like we know our blades melt the ice). When I'm skating, I don't have to worry about my body and who might like to kiss me. I don't worry about who I like, or who I *should* like. And not a single skater—not Winnie, not any of my skating partners—has noticed that I choreograph different types of dance numbers, different skating "steps," depending on who my dance partner is. Or maybe they've noticed, but think I'm just tweaking the routine to fit the skater. But I'm not, I'm changing the routine to fit *me*, to fit how much (or little) I'd like the other skater to fit me.

Truth be true, at skating practice, I let it all hang out there, baby (Austin Powers cracks me up). And not a single one of those straight girls (oh, trust me, they're all het-girl straight) ever figures out my devious plans. I'm not surprised the other skaters don't realize that I'm choreographing dance routines just to get some of their hands on my hips, but I'm disappointed Sita hasn't got my number yet. Sita is crack-the-whip smart, yet she hasn't put the puzzle together. She hasn't noticed that my puzzles come with five corner pieces or with too few straight-edged pieces to make the dream-teen picture. That's because I've become an expert at keeping all the different puzzle pieces in separate piles. Separate boxes, even. In separate galaxies.

❄

Tonight at supper, the parentals have gotten under Tyler's skin and he whispers, "I wish I could pack you two in a crate and ship you out to Vancouver ..." When my mom stops pouring water and my dad stops scraping the last of the leftover stir-fry onto his plate, Turd realizes his whisper hasn't even been close to a "whis." But does he stop? Oh no. "Where your hippie friends have all gathered for the great unpacking."

He slurps the last of the rice noodles and tosses his fork onto his plate. Astoundingly, my mother laughs. My dad, too, but his bray is a few beats behind my mother's. He clutches at his own fork a little too tightly to make me believe he enjoys the joke. Still, he does laugh, so Turd is off the hook.

But Samantha isn't.

"Hippies from Vancouver!" she yells and clanks down her fork.

"Manners," Mom admonishes.

"Little Miss," my father co-admonishes. "You're going to have to learn how to behave like a proper lady at the supper table if you ever want to be a guest in someone's house."

My parents often punish Sam—nothing too serious, cuz she's, like, seven—but it does seem like Sam gets it more than anyone else. I tap one of her wheels under the table with my big toe to let her know it's okay.

"Do *not* kick Samantha's chair!" Mom bellows. Like I'm the ogre. Whatever.

My father just slams back his chair and leaves the room, without even a single "hasta la vista."

Whatever, *squared*.

Tyler makes it up to Sammie by agreeing to play her favourite card game after supper with us. In the middle of our second game, Sam calls "Cheat!" because Tyler claims he's got all four Jacks. In

Cheat, the point is to cheat, but if you get caught, you end up with more and more cards. Whoever's out of cards first wins.

Sammie shuffles her three remaining cards then announces, "Three Queens." The odds of Sam having three Queens right when it's her turn to bet Queens is way too lucky. But Sammie never cheats. Never. That's how she always wins.

"Cheat!" Tyler shouts, falling for her ruse, and Sam flips over the Queen of Hearts, Queen of Spades, and Queen of Clubs. So Tyler has to pick up her cards *and* the rest of the pile. The rules say he and I should play on to see who comes in second, but: *No way, José. Not a chance, Lance.* When Sammie wins, the game is done, and we pack up for bed.

LESBO ALERT: BECAUSE OF SKATING, SHE WEARS HER HAIR DEAD-SHORT.

HET-GIRL ALERT: BECAUSE OF SKATING, SHE WEARS CUTESY SKIRTS.

CHAPTER SEVEN

As I'm usually up eons before she is, Sita often awakes to a text from me. "gud morn! grab a latte for me b4 bell?" or: "S, r u ready 4 test?" and I go to bed with advice about how I should skip icicle practice tomorrow and join her in watching grade ten boys zip through the library because they're trying to avoid grade twelve boys or a description of the length to which her parents went over her math homework, even though the answers are in the back of the book. Sita's texts sometimes continue onto a part two and sometimes even a part three.

Yes, I've been a complete coward about outing myself to my best friend. But as we start our third week of school, I'm still hoping to confess my summer news. I get dressed in a rush, rush through skating practice ("This is not a race, Keira," shouts Winnie. "We're not speed-skating here!"), and rush through breakfast back home. Despite all my hurry, I'm late and only get to school by the second, tardy, bell. Tomorrow, I pledge, tomorrow we'll have a real chat. Once I talk to Sita, really talk to her, then that will be it. Problem is, I really don't know the best way to tell the story of this summer. After I own up to kissing Surge, I'll be set as a het-girl.

"Just decide," someone on one of the "bi-curious" websites advised. "Don't wimp out by pretending you like everyone." I *don't* like everyone, but why do I have to like only *one kind of* someone? Sita and I always talk about boys. Always. So depending on how I tell her my news, there might not be any wiggle room any more.

I know some boys get weirded out about how much girls tell each other, but without Sita's background information, I would be lost, lost, lost about how to behave around boys. Even loster than I am. Because when you're basically a virgin, it actually helps quite a bit if your best friend is a dating expert. Or at least if she thinks she is and so has already navigated the whole "Are we ready to plunge into *that?*" thing.

"Don't let them pressure you," she advised me the first time we had a conversation about going all the way. At this point, most sex was way "academic" for both of us. We were in grade seven. I had a crush on Tommy Ito, mainly because he played the saxophone and stood in front of me during band practice. Sita had been dating since grade five. She'd already made it to second base with three of her boyfriends, and we were discussing whether or not she should try for third.

She lay down on her back, and spoke to the sky. "But we're not talking about going-all-the-way sex, here. We're talking about when you should let guys push you into doing something—anything—you don't want to do. You know when? Never." She licked her popsicle, making the lick as dirty as possible, and I cracked up.

Sita's three older sisters all used to brag to baby sis about their boyfriends. And gave details about length of kiss (looooong), where hands should go (inside the shirt, but above the waist), and how far to go with a boy (never as far as they suggest). Sita even spied on some of these real-world boys kissing her sisters. I tried licking my popsicle in a dirty way, too, but just got orange goop in my nostril. That cracked *her* up.

She continued with the sex lecture. "Look, be yourself because, well, there isn't really anybody else to be. If you pretend you like the band Cum4tMe, which you actually hate, just to impress a guy who's really into that band, you're gonna have to listen to that music for the next hundred and five dates in a row." She rolled onto her side so we were facing each other.

I really did detest Cum4tMe, and the idea of one of their songs repeating over and over and over inside shared earplugs did kinda depress me. But how was I supposed to talk about things like music with boys? At that point in junior high school, the only songs I really knew well were skating songs.

Sita reached out for my arm, as if she were about to impart some serious medical advice. "Look, it's way less complicated to just say what you think, feel what you feel, and hope the two of you click. If you don't, well, better off discovering that after a couple of dates than after you've been going out for a year!"

She rolled onto her back again, and I took the (nearly) true confession plunge: "I've got a crush on Tommy Ito." Way back then, I knew I had crushes on girls too, but I thought (assumed? hoped?) they'd go away. That having a crush on a boy meant I still had a chance at being a *real* girl.

"Tommy may be cute, and he might be a fab kisser. But you're not gonna find out by pretending you like sticking your tongue deep into his left nostril when all you want is for him to melt his bottom lip over your top one." I snorted at that. Then I admitted that we'd held hands once in the library, but nothing since then.

"Maybe he's a homo." Sita said "homo" like it was some rare type of frog. Like something you'd dissect in science class. Something *other* people are, not anyone we'd ever get to know.

"Sita—that's so *rude*." I sat up abruptly, wiping imaginary grass stains off my knees and shins.

"Is *not*. You said you guys held hands and now you don't. You didn't even lock lips. Straight guys want to kiss the girls they hug. He did hug you, right?" She tapped my elbow to check, as if I'd maybe got part of my own story wrong.

"You think any guy who might be interested in me has to be gay? Why would you say—"

"What?" She must have heard the panic in my voice because her next question was, "Are you afraid of being gay?"

"Don't be an idjit," was my answer then. Anything to escape that conversation without honestly answering her question. I wonder, though: if Sita asked me now, what would I say?

We've had versions of this conversation for about three years. She tells me about her latest guy, and I have to say, for the most part, I like them. They're not at all like the rabid take-what-they-can-get boys she's always warning me about. Perhaps it's something about her sisters' boyfriends? Unlike Tyler, they're friendly—as friendly as a guy who's four or five years older can be. They say hello, we chat about what courses they're taking in university, they grab a granola bar, and then exit. Freakin' friendly, compared with my older sibling.

Sita puts up with my passion for swirling around on top of frozen water ("frozen *dirty* water," she once sniffed). She likes Sam, doesn't let Tyler get under her skin, and manages to impress my parents with her university-aimed goals. No matter that those goals are her *parents'*. Sita never abandons me when she has a boyfriend, and she gives me embarrassing details about what the two of them do together (like what goes where and for how long). But I've never given her any specific sex stuff about myself since that grade seven "confession," because one tiny detail might lead to another bigger detail and next thing I know, I'll be telling her I daydream about girls. Sometimes. This is why the Surge confession is so hard—how do I tell Sita without telling her everything? Do I want to tell her everything?

Looks like I have two problems: A) what if my best friend freaks out that I'm not trying out for the all-het boy-crazy girls' club? and B) what if she doesn't, but then is furious because I've never confessed to her before, even though she confesses *everything* to me? Yikes. Double-whammy best-friend conundrum.

This third Friday of high school, we've settled into our regular coffee shop and our regular conversation topic. Sita starts with Daz, who volunteers at Planet Philosophy, working to make the city more bike-friendly. His car-free plans make Sita swoon. She actually says "swoon." Then we discuss the possibility of me—finally, finally, finally—hooking up with some guy. By now, my loveless love life is so tragic that Sita says I should take *anyone* for my first kiss. Hmmmm. I bend my head and slurp the last of my latte foam.

HET-GIRL ALERT: OF **COURSE** SHE'S AFRAID OF BEING LABELLED AS GAY, OF ANYONE THINKING SHE **MIGHT** BE GAY, OF THINKING SHE'D EVER JOIN THE GREAT BIG GAY CLUB IN THE SKY!

LESBO ALERT: OF **COURSE** SHE'S AFRAID OF ANYONE FINDING OUT SHE MIGHT BE GAY.

CHAPTER EIGHT

September's settling down. Homework, lunchtime with Sita and Amanda (and "The Three"), Friday afternoons with just Sita and me, figure skating every morning, part-time jobs, studying, and evenings with Sammie. And there are assignments and quizzes that I absca-ma-lute-ly have to get fairly good grades in. The Regionals skating competition is the first weekend in November, and I need to nail that in order to concentrate on the Provincial Finals at the end of January.

So spare me the lecture, Mom. She thinks now that I'm in high school, maybe she and I should have a regular study date so I can begin to prep for university. Her idea is that she'll leave the office an hour early on Fridays, cuz things slow down right before the weekend. I'm supposed to give up my *one* free slot of friendship time to study? For university? With my mother? *Forget that, Matt!* I'm only in grade ten—uni is, like, three years from now. My parents crossed the country right after graduation, leaving everyone they knew behind. Maybe her high school friends weren't important to *her*, but mine sure are to me.

This particular argument is taking place while we're shopping for groceries. Sammie's zooming ahead, clearing the aisles so our cart can breeze along freely. This is her favourite shopping chore. That, and piling licorice into the cart (did I tell you I'm allergic to licorice?) without the Mom Police noticing. No point in me asking for snacks in the grocery store; that's what job money is for. Besides, Mom and I have enough to argue about.

"Look, Mom, after high school, Sita's going to follow her many siblings into university." So far, so good. My parents already think Sita's a brainiac (which she is) and that her ambitions will rub off on me.

I toss some frozen spinach into the cart to impress her with my dedication to all things healthy. Mom puts the package back in the freezer, saying, "Stick to the grocery list, please, Keira."

"So listen, she and I will study together. Sita needs to keep her grades high," I point out, "so Fridays won't always be just lattes and gossip." Uh-oh, even mentioning the things you're convincing your parents you *won't* do reminds them about their concerns. "I promise." And then I add, "Don't forget our B-plus school/job deal."

We're in line, and Mom's going over every item in the cart to add them up before we get to the cashier. *Embarrassing*—doesn't she trust the automatic tills? Sammie zooms through an empty cashier and waits for us by the doors, thrumming her wheel-spokes, making up a song: "You guys take too long / Longer than this song / Get a move along." I'll say this for Mom, though: like me, she can do all the calculating in her head, no pencil. Maybe *she* should go to university instead.

The worst thing about Mom is that she's rigid: she does *not* like to change her mind. But you can work that in your favour, too. We had a deal about grades so unless I don't hold up my end, she has to give me my one day a week. I'll get through high school with passable grades because that is my parents' decree. But if I get into university, what *will* I do? I'm good at math, but that doesn't lead to jobs any more than professional skating does. The cashier looks up right then and nods at me, as if we know each other, as if I'm already her work-buddy.

By the time we get home, Mom's dropped this particular conversation, at least for now, to focus on dinner preparations.

✳

End of September, and Sita and I are already talking about the Hallowe'en dance. We walk out of the cafeteria wrapped up in a discussion of costumes and cliques and my constant complaint about a certain older sibling. We're not really paying attention to which kids are still in the cafeteria. There are two lunch supervisors and two teachers assigned as guards, but that still makes about 350 kids per four adults. You do the math.

I'm in the middle of mentioning that slow dancing with Brady Campbell—even if he was wrapped in a Dracula cape—would be way too yucky an experience for me. He's on, like, every team the school has. But from what Tyler told Sammie last night, Brady never showers—not even after gym class or football games. "Probably not even in the morning in his own house," said Tyler.

This is what I'm telling Sita as we exit the cafeteria when—thwack—I get hit on the shoulder. Caramel pudding. I turn to gloop it off and glare at whichever idjit flung it there. Probably Tyler, impressing his friends. But no, it's Jason Billings, who I'd always thought was kinda cute, even if he's got a dump truck of a personality. Tyler slaps him on the back, and Jason waggles his tongue at me. He knows I can't fling anything back and I can't shout anything either, as Sita and I are right by the doors. The teachers may be busy chatting with each other instead of monitoring the room, but they can still hear.

So I let it pass. At least the bell hasn't rung yet. Sita walks with me to the washroom and stands guard while I take off my shirt and scrub the neon-brown stain with industrial-strength institution soap. Now it just looks like Barbie threw up on my shoulder. Or worse than threw up.

"Starting tomorrow," I announce, "I'm keeping an extra set of clothes in my locker." I button up the shirt, motioning to Sita that she can unguard the door.

"Hey, good idea, let's go," she says, pulling my arm as the first bell rings.

"Wait!" I pull back. "Let me get under the hand-dryer for a minute." I scrunch down, trying to position my shoulder for maximum drying.

"No time, we have to get to the gym lockers." She's still tugging. "Come on." She yanks really hard, and I fly toward her. "You can use your gym top. It may be a bit stinky, but at least it's not *radiant khaki*."

That was Tuesday. On Wednesday, we walk out of the cafeteria backward, nearly tripping over the six volleyballs that mysteriously materialized there. Tyler and Jason again, though what Jason's getting out of all this is beyond me. Maybe the grade twelves feel they didn't have a good enough run with us tenth graders during Frosh Week and have extended the torture period? More likely Tyler just gets off on causing me public humiliation, and Jason loves the ride. Point is, this all takes place in the cafeteria, so lots of other jerks start to notice. And not just the jerks, but everyone. Bad news if you're busy trying to be invisible.

On Thursday, Talia Sitkins accidentally sprays the shower at my back after I've already changed out of my gym clothes. I get soaked, but I have actually remembered to bring an extra shirt to keep in my locker, so it's no big deal.

"This is a big deal," Sita says, as she walks me to an extra skating practice on Thursday after supper. She won't stay and watch, but the rink isn't far from her place, and she *does* attend my competitions.

"Talia Sitkins is such a follower!" I spit out. "She'll do anything anybody tells her to do, even ride her bike over her own mother." I have more things to say about Talia, but aiming your shower at a girl just because her brother is already making her life miserable is just too junior high. Talia Sitkins doesn't warrant further discussion. We're almost at the rink, so we both instinctively slow down. Winnie won't love it if I'm late, but I am adding these extra Thursday practices, so she won't complain too much.

"Exactly," says Sita. "It's not just Tyler and his goons any more. You have to take action." Like we're in a Hollywood flick, like we're cops or tough guys. Maybe Sita expects me to fling my skates at somebody.

"I know how to deal with Tyler," I reassure her. "He only likes to bug me if it bugs me. That's why he got Jason to fling the food, pitch the pudding, toss the tapioca—" Sita stops walking and so I stop alliterating. "Point is, he'll stop."

"No. The point is, it's not Tyler any more. It's the sheep like Talia Sitkins. If the sheep think you're a target, a safe target, this will go on for weeks. Maybe longer." She looks so grim, I'm impressed.

"Okay," I tell her, though I'm not sure what I'm agreeing to.

"Okay." I head in to the rink, and Sita heads back home. But we've agreed to something, some plan Sita is already hatching in her adorable brain, which we put the final touches on while texting that night.

Friday, we wait till last bell. Sita's wearing a rose-coloured blouse and matching shoes. I'm wearing a loose, taupe jersey and I put extra gel in my hair, like I do on competition days. Today is a high-adrenalin day. On the way to my locker, I clip Tyler on the shoulder as I run past—a fast slap that he barely acknowledges, as if a feeble girl-hit is exactly the kind of retaliation he expects from his dweeb little sister. Tyler's wearing his fave "I'm prettier than you are" T-shirt. There are just enough kids around to enjoy this little play that Sita has scripted for our after-school pleasure.

Behind me I hear Tyler's friends burst into laughter at the "PITY ME: I'M TYLER'S TWIN" message I've taped onto his back. He turns around to give me the finger, but I ignore him to enjoy the rest of the show.

As soon as Tyler rips the sign off his back, the crowd is already hooting again, this time at Jason. While I'm running past Tyler, Sita's casually loitering around, slapping Jason's back like he's been brilliant all week attacking her best friend. She even bats her eyes at him, I swear. And Jason drinks it in. He's cute, but not the sharpest fork in the cutlery drawer. His sign reads: "I CAN'T READ EITHER."

As Sita struts casually away from the circle of braying hyenas, Jason begins to figure out that Tyler isn't our only target. He whips his head around, like he's able to see over his shoulder, and then yanks at the paper. Unlike Tyler, Jason holds it right in front of his face, reading it through a couple of times.

"I don't get it," I hear him say, to further hoots. Boy, am I gonna get it over the weekend. Totally, totally worth it.

I'll say this for Tyler, he's a total twerp, but he's not a baby. He crumples up Jason's sign and throws it on the floor next to his. "Let's go," he jerks his head at the boy horde.

"Bitches!" Jason calls out.

At that, Tyler whirls around and slugs Jason for insulting his sister.

Ha, ha, as if.

"I said, let's go," he repeats and heads off down the hall with anyone who'll follow. Most of the grade twelves do.

Not Jason.

Sita, who doesn't hurry, reaches halfway to where I'm standing when Jason starts after her. For a second I think he's going to hit her, but even Jason must be smart enough to know that hitting a girl for teasing you is a sure-fire ticket to Loser City. A few kids are still hanging around, waiting to see what Jason's up to.

"Slag!" Jason calls out at Sita, the word bouncing off the metal lockers, giving the sound a metallic jangle. Slag? A useless insult—who outside of British television ever uses that word?

Jason must have been playing for time, though, because he doesn't say anything else until he's standing directly in front of Sita. She goes to walk around him, still heading down the hallway toward me, but he blocks her way, pushes his chest at hers. And then I get it: Jason hasn't been picking on us all week just because I'm Tyler's sister: he's been trying to get Sita's attention. And now she's called him an idjit in front of his friends.

"You don't have to be like that," he says. "We weren't after *you*." His big flirt move. Guess when you're that good-looking, you don't have to foster much charm.

"Mmm?" she responds. As in, "go on."

"Well, you're cute, in a *foreign* kind of a way." Jason swirls his hips, emphasizing that what he says is a compliment. Except I can't tell if he's seriously hitting on her or just randomly insulting her. "You're like, you know, exotic, and good for a, well—"

I don't think Sita has worked out if he's for real, either, because this time when she says, "Go on," it's to make him speak the words he's thinking. Would he really stoop that low?

Now's the time to mention that one of the reasons Sita and I have lasted as best friends is that we're both really good at standing our ground and sticking up for the right thing. For each other, I mean. We both totally suck at sticking up for ourselves.

With Jason blocking her way and flinging insults at her face, Sita's shoulders just hunch down, which means she's not going to let her talent for being adorable get her out of this one. She could smile up at him, as if she were shy. She could do the hand-wave thing, dismissing him and saving herself. But she doesn't do any of those things. She's not even looking at Jason any more, but off to his right, as if to measure how far she's standing from the next set of doors. A long way. Even if she runs now, his ugly words will hit her square on the shoulders as she races away.

"Don't you finish that sentence, Jason Billings!" I yell out. Not that I think I'll be able to stop him, but at least he won't be able to whisper racist shit into Sita's ear without witnesses. The few kids left in the hallways stop pretending to twirl their locks, and just face the action.

Jason knows that Tyler won't care one bit if he tears me to strips in front of the entire school. But Jason isn't interested in me. Not any more. He only has eyes for Sita. And Sita only has eyes for the linoleum floor.

"Stay out of this, *princess!*" Jason shoots over his shoulder at me. "This is between me and the brown girl."

Jason hasn't yet said the worst word, the one he's building up to, but the way he says "brown" makes it sound important—in a rotten way. A way that's hard to pinpoint, but so easy to *feel*. Sita, who never takes shit from anyone, just stands there taking it.

I walk up to them and stand behind him. He doesn't even bother to turn. One advantage of being a tall girl is that you're about the same height as most boys in grade twelve. I quietly place my feet about three inches behind his and position my knees behind his.

"That's *Ice* Princess, to you, jerk!" I yell into his ear, bending my knees forward and making his buckle. He grabs for Sita, but she ducks to the side, so it looks like he's lunging at her but misses. "And right now," I yell, "the *brown* girl and the *white* girl have much, MUCH better things to do than hang around in the hallways with a *red-letter* boy." His football jacket has "JB" embroidered on the chest.

Sita chortles (you know, chokes *and* snorts at the same time). Maybe because calling someone a red-letter-boy is as ridiculous as thinking that "brown" is an insult. Maybe because Jason now needs the floor more than she did. "Which one of us is the white girl again?" she asks, hooking her arm around mine.

"That bitch to your left," Jason sneers, peeling his knees off the floor. "The Ice Princess," and he says it just like he'd said the word "brown." Suddenly my retort is smudged and aimed back at me. I really hadn't thought that Jason would immediately make it into a sex joke. Or did he?

I decide that his repeating my term mostly reminds everyone that I had a pretty good comeback for him. So today, with our little morality play, Sita and I actually win.

IDJIT ALERT: JASON—SOMEONE-LEFT-THE-TAP-ON-TOO-LONG—BILLINGS (NUF SAID!).

CHAPTER NINE

The first thing that gets you when your skates hit the ice is *not* the cold. No, morning rinks woo us skaters. Because the Zamboni has washed the ice with a thin sheen of water, paving over all hockey games and open-skate practices from the day before. That's what gets me up when the alarm blares, gets me out the door on a glacier of a day like today.

In summer, it's kinda great to have what feels like air conditioning built-in, though in the dead of winter, we all want to drag electric heaters onto the rink with us. But that's usually only a few months of every year. September and October, March and April—for the most part—are fine. Today is *not* fine. Sometimes, Alberta gets fabulous, magical warmth in the middle of winter because of Chinooks. These warm winds blow in and last either a few hours or a week. People walk around in February wearing shorts and T-shirts. For skaters, the Chinooks totally help to relax a body that's been strained and clenched by deep, deep winter. But today, I think as I leave the house into what feels like the middle of night, today must be the opposite of a Chinook. We've had a freak fall snowstorm, and the days are filled with icicle-drenched air.

Doesn't help that on Friday morning, we're into minus-minus weather, yet I can still taste summer (well, Surge) on my lips! But memories of blueberries and burnt marshmallows fade too quickly with this temp drop. Carrying my skates, the laces feel frozen solid already. Maybe the gods are giving me a sign. Maybe it's time to become a gymnast, where you practice indoors, where your fingers are never too cold to lace up your dainty gymnast booties. Ha.

By the time I trudge into the change room at the community centre, my bones are joined-together ice cubes. Then we have to take off our winter coats and toasty boots and slip our feet into not-so-toasty toe-torture machines. Usually Winnie lets us practice in double layers of long underwear, though sometimes we have to wear our competition outfits, short skirts and thin nylons. Those days, she yells, "Skate fast and you'll stay warm!" even though she's usually yelling at us to "Slow down! It's not a race!" And, yes, she walks around the ice in lined boots and wrapped tightly in her winter coat.

But once I'm ready to go, the first thing that sends a thrill up my spine is the gorgeous, pristine ice. At this time of day, not a single skater has marked it up. We're the first since the Zamboni smoothed over all the rough patches the night before. I push off from the boards, glide to the centre, and stand with my feet in a T-formation, hands on my hips. Then, even though Winnie absolutely insists we begin with warm-up figure 8s, I do a short warm-up routine, starting with the opening I'm planning for the Regional competition. It's slow, but each turn builds on the last, each jump shoots my legs higher, and each spin whips my head faster and faster. I really, really should start with my figures, but having the entire rink to myself is too tempting. When I try the triple Lutz, I land a bit too sharply on the edge of my blade and nearly topple over. Still worth it.

Yep, *this* is why I skate, why I get up at rooster hour, freeze my butt (quite often fall on my butt), have to rush home from the arena and then rush to school, have to scrub dental gunk for extra cash so

I can afford quality skates, so I can afford the fee to enter the competition, so I can afford to get to the competitions. The ice is so immaculate, I can believe the blemishes I make are all perfect, that my routine is the finest it can get, that the music I've chosen and my routine will fuse in my body. Not a single rough patch. The ice itself will lift me when I need to reach high and guide me when I'm in danger of falling. Yeah, I know: figure-skating nerd.

This moment is why I never join in when the other skaters complain that we get the worst ice hours, that the only thing our community cares about is hockey, hockey, hockey. I think our community cares just as little about girls' hockey, though, so I guess we should count ourselves lucky. I finish off with a double Axel, skid without falling, and finally start to outline two fat circles with the outside of my blade. I don't mind figure 8s, though most of the other skaters do.

"But we don't need to do them in a competition, Winnie," Zoë Bandicoff whines. Zoë's a bit of a whiner. Winnie's always lecturing us about how when she was competing, they not only had to practice their figure 8s, but half the actual competition was judged on them. The audience could watch a brilliant dance routine, see a skater get near-perfect scores from all the judges, and still come in seventh place—all because she'd blown her figures.

Zoë hates doing figures because her 8s look more like dented letter Bs. She's the best jumper of all of us, but she's all force, all show. She's never bought second-hand skates in her life, her parents eagerly purchase extra ice time, private coaching, three glitzy competition outfits. But Zoë doesn't get that bling doesn't matter, not the way figure 8s do.

Don't get me wrong. I adore flying through a routine, lifting my leg higher with a hefty skate strapped to my foot than I ever could if I was just standing around in sneakers. But there's something peaceful about drawing a thin circle in the pristine ice, then going over and over and over that circle—inside blade and then outside blade—without making the outline of the circle barely any thicker, without changing the formula. Without ever reaching an end.

When I skate, I can be me: enjoying myself, calculating the height I need for this jump, the width I need for that twirl, challenging myself, my only worry being falling onto my *toujours*-tender tush (take that, Mr Grier, alliteration *and* Franglais!). When I'm skating, I get to just be in my body, no either/or choices.

The point of figure skating isn't getting there first; that would be speed skating. The point of figure skating isn't looking grandiose and glorious; that would be the Ice Capades.

Zoë can leap around like the air has footholds for her to catch onto, but it's not enough. I'm good enough to keep wanting to win, but I'd skate anyway, even if I didn't have a hope of placing at the National Finals. That's how Tyler and I differ. Gliding through freezing air and onto the ice makes my heart melt. Winning at football makes his heart race. He even has good-luck rituals and routines he taps out before every game. Zoë's the same way: she thinks kissing her snowflake bracelet will help gain her a medal. For me, all of it matters: the skating and twirling and figure-8-ing.

I don't even mind that I'm late for school—again. Classes at J.J. Backstrom start twenty minutes earlier than they did at our junior high, and I still haven't worked out how to give up those twenty minutes of extra dreaming at the crack of dawn.

As of today, we've survived a month of high school. The semester is in full swing: clubs, football, homework, even mid-terms loom. I haven't exactly aced my assignments so far, but I've done well enough that I don't have to start panicking until November. Which means, Sita informs me, that we have time for the "get Keira a boyfriend" plan. Gulp.

I give her my list: "Max Bledsoe, Rick from math (seriously yummy forearms!), the Trevor without a car (he cycles to school even in winter), and Marly." The last name just slips out. Have I done it, have I finally confessed my inner desires to my best friend?

"*What?!*" she questions me, and at first I think her shock is because I find one of Joline's minions attractive. Yeah, Marly's personality may be robot-like, but her lips are pretty juicy. But, nope, Sita's shock goes in a different direction: "Like as in, *Marty Ghanem*? You have a crush on one of your brother's jock-pals?" Her shock turns sour: "He's enough of a goon to turn any girl lesbo!" At that, my mouth clamps down and stays clamped. We immediately turn to her list.

At that party we crashed, Sita flirted with Tony Baloney (what, you think I'm the only one with a doofus nickname?), but ended up in the backyard with Daz, who's in grade eleven and cool enough to be invited to the party, but enough of a culture-geek to also be in the Drama Club.

"Daz deliberately doesn't comb his hair sometimes," Sita confesses to me just before ordering her second double mocha. "He says you have to be careful sometimes if you're into drama and a guy."

Her words convince me *not* to come out to Sita. Because how am I supposed to respond? That I agree being in Drama Club and being a straight guy is a hardship? That all "fags" like acting? How can I deal with these hardee-har comments out the mouth of my best friend? I'm articulate enough *inside* my head, but out in the open I can only sputter. Usually, I'm just tongue-tied.

"I'm thinking of getting a buzz-cut," I announce. As a counter or maybe to introduce my topic in an obviously too subtle way? But Sita doesn't bite. Either she doesn't believe me or she does but doesn't allow this info to derail what she's been saying about Daz.

"Daz gets any part that demands singing or yodeling," she continues. You'd be surprised how many school plays demand yodeling. As Sita's loyal fan, I've suffered through a lot. "Or long memorization." She stops for a second, then continues once I've finished swallowing. "You know what that means, don't you?"

What, she's worried I'm not paying attention? Or has Sita finally noticed how one-sided these conversations are?

"What I'm telling you is that Daz was the lead boy for every performance last year."

Ah, and Sita wants to play opposite him. For more than one reason, now. Even before the party, Sita was gunning for lead girl. As a grade ten newbie, she barely has a hope of snagging it. But Sita wants the dazzling boy *and* a dazzling role. In that order.

"Given what the drama teacher has lined up, though, I think Daz will get called a 'homo' this year, for sure." And there it is: Sita's big worry for her new darling.

Homo. That word, again. Why? Tyler's not actually out every

night with a different girl; he's out every night with the same set of (jock-boy) friends. Hanging out. But nobody's calling Tyler and his friends homos. Except each other. As a joke. A joke that's hilarious because—obviously—no cool teenage jock would ever be a homo. No, that special label is saved for the chess players and drama geeks, the math geniuses, and even guys in the Film Buffs Club.

The coffee shop is mostly filled with groups, not couples. Shit on a stick, how could Sita spit out the word "homo" as if she's spitting sunflower seeds from her lips? Talia Sitkins and friends have taken over a table not far from ours. They each wear pleated skirts, which is maybe a club thing or maybe just coordinated fashion. Because of what I see on the ice day-in, day-out, I don't find heavy skirts particularly attractive. Doesn't mean I can stop my mind from thinking about what's underneath those skirts. Good thing Sita can't read my thoughts. Most of the time.

"Look, can we walk around a bit?" I ask. "I know it's Arctic weather out there, but the company in here's getting kinda stuffy."

We grab our bags and transfer from mugs to paper. Sita will allow to-go cups as long as we recycle when we're done. It would be easy to change the topic now, but something inside me doesn't want to.

"So, what's the diff if Daz gets called a homo or one of the 'gay' guys in drama?"

"Because the gay guys are homos. Duh." Hand wave. I chew on the paper cup while Sita delivers boring Drama Club info about soft costumes and stiff ghosts from past performances. I'm already regretting our move outside; neither of us have worn scarves, or even decent jackets.

Our school's first production, *I Am a Camera*, is scheduled to co-incide with Hallowe'en. Except it took the Drama Club forever to get permission from the principal to put on a production that inspired the musical *Cabaret*. Which is hilarious because if they'd just asked to do *Cabaret*, they probably would have gotten permission, no problem. Sita's dying to play Sally Bowles, especially with Daz as the obvious choice for male lead.

Sita tells me that she's told Daz about how she and Lucien made out before school started—even though it was a summer fling and barely lasted two minutes. Her reasoning? "I tell the truth, for Krishna's sake!"

Lucien isn't into Drama Club, and he isn't a jock, either. He's the good-looking guy who melts your knees when you walk by him and he smiles. And he almost always smiles. Tyler's friend Jason is cute but would climb over dead bodies to get ahead. Lucien is sort of the opposite. He's *nice*. Really nice. He talks to grade ten kids, he lets anyone join a conversation he's in. He makes out with my best friend in early August. He just doesn't do the long-term relationship. Lucien's rumoured agenda is to sleep with a hundred girls by the time he graduates from high school. And he actually tells girls this. Instead of being the school creep, he comes off as honest and direct. Funny thing is, most girls respect him. It's the boys who can't stand Luscious Lucien.

"I told Daz about Lucien because I want him to know I've been with a pretty great kisser, but that I choose *him*."

"Um, that's how you put it to him?" I ask. I'm no expert, but letting your new boyfriend know you're still daydreaming about your most recent kiss-buddy can't be the way to secure his heart. But then, what do I know about securing anybody's heart? I haven't even had a text from Surge in a couple of weeks.

Sita just shrugs. "I also told Daz about Lucien because I want him to trust me. He doesn't have to, but I'm not going to beg him to." And that statement defines Sita in a nutshell: She's boy-crazy, but she also wants a guy who thinks she's a catch, not a consolation prize. She wants to be lead girl in all the school plays, wants to date the lead boy, and wants her boyfriend to be grade eleven Daz-the-Jazz. But if none of that is enough for Daz, he's just gonna have to live without her.

Even though it's only early October, today is so ridiculously cold that we end up just walking home. Sita takes my empty cup when we part at her place. We don't see each other all weekend because of our crazy schedules, but I figure out that Daz must have got a similar lecture, because next thing you know, Sita and Daz get caught in a serious make-out session behind the scenery in the drama room.

Not only does the drama teacher catch them, but at least five kids who walk in with the teacher see the porn flick. When they turn on the lights, Daz runs out, abandoning Sita with her sweater up around her neck.

And then today, the school's incredibly efficient gossip machine is fuelled by a note Jason Billings very deliberately passes during his grade twelve Social Studies class. Jason is obviously itching for Mr Rempel to lend weight to the note by snatching it out of his hand. He does, but not before eight kids have already read it and passed it along. It doesn't even have a destination. Just Sita's name, and "S-L-U-T" in curlicue letters beneath.

One night of snow, and the city is covered in white. Flakes are still coming down when I walk to skating practice in the morning. My footsteps are the first on the block, the first to reach the community centre. The weather is totally ridic, but it's also magic. It's minus twenty-seven Celsius in the sun, which means if you're me and late getting into the shower after you get home from skating, you have to run to school with wet hair. By the time I arrive, my hair ends have frozen into tiny pointy icicle formations, like I'm a punk '80s girl, which I am *so* not.

"Hey, it's the Ice Princess," Max Bledsoe comments when I walk into Social Studies just as the second bell rings. It's like he's invented a whole new punchline today. Like he's funny. The entire class hoots. I guess nicknames never get old.

"People!" calls out Mr Rempel, and we get down to studying the impact of globalization on local economies. Sita is in that class, but Rumpled makes us sit in alphabetical order, and that puts us diagonally across the room from each other. She fiddles with her elegant (read: *dry*) hair to show sympathy for my now dripping mop. By the time we open our books to the chapter on tourism, my stalactites have become a stringy mess.

Jason Billings is a jerk, but he was really risking his life with that note. Nobody passes notes in front of Mr Rempel. Or behind his back for that matter, not unless they really, *really* want trouble. His nickname may be Rumpled, but it's because he's Mr Straight-and-Narrow when it comes to students behaving in his class. Jason didn't just get detention for a week, he got suspended from the football team for one game. Another reason to hate us. To hate Sita.

Sita and I don't even wave when the bell rings, just rush to the next war zone. None of the teachers are as scary as Rempel, but high school definitely feels like it's "us against them." We don't see each other for three classes.

"Come out to the east foyer, I want to talk." She grabs me at lunchtime as I'm heading to our usual table. Amanda is nowhere in sight. Joline and The Two have already slumped past us on the way to the library. Marly looked pretty cute in a retro bowling jacket, but she doesn't notice me, and I pretend not to notice her chest. Sita knows I have a bag lunch, so we don't need to eat in the cafeteria. So I grab my two egg sandwiches and two mango juice boxes and follow her.

I assume she wants to talk about getting me my first kiss. I'm getting truly sick of only talking about half of my wish-kiss list (less than half, since girls outnumber boys on that list). I still can't predict which girls might like me or why, but what I could do is tell Sita which ones I like. I start to twitch at the thought of saying, "Actually, Sita, my list is longer than you think. A *lot* longer," but even when they stay inside my head the words sound loud. Too loud.

One whisper to Sita and the whole school would know. Not that she'd tell. But too many secrets sort of seep through the school walls. If I say *I like girls*, to anyone, I'll be labelled and pegged and cursed. If I ever say those words out loud—even if I'm standing there alone, breathing sub-zero carbon dioxide out into the bright, harsh air—someone will hear. And spread the news that the Ice Princess is the

Ice Queen (or is that just a word for gay guys?).

Still, not telling Sita feels like lying. And since the summer, that feeling is growing—every time we have a heart-to-heart (her heart to my half-hearted). Problem is, I still haven't figured out a way to map out the words in my head. Like designing a skating routine, I need to know what I'll say to Sita before I say it. So I twitch at her request, but I pretend it's only from the cold as we leave the school.

"Daz and I broke up," she says as soon as the door closes behind us. "He left me to face the masses by myself." Normally, about two dozen kids huddle around the east foyer, but today's too cold even for the smokers, so we have the grounds to ourselves.

"Cuz of the rumours?" What kind of jerk is Daz turning out to be?

"Nope, he says he can't get over me making out with Lucien. He can't stop worrying that it was more than just kissing." She slaps the brick wall, as if hitting something will help, but she doesn't slap that hard. She's angry at him, but obviously on the edge of forgiveness. "And I know it's a lousy thing, but oh my god, Lucien kisses like his name sounds, and Daz, well ..."

"Kisses like his name sounds?" I finish for her.

"Actually, Daz has gotten better. Slower. He thinks about my mouth and not just his tongue in it." She shrugs. "You think I'm an idjit?"

"I think these walls gossip about us behind our backs," I say, slapping the frozen bricks myself. Then I breathe into my cupped hands. "But I don't think Daz said anything to Jason, if that's what you're asking."

That's what she's asking. Sita knows who she wants to kiss and why. She knows which guy she's willing to get to various bases with, and she doesn't like or dislike a boy because of his popularity rating. But no matter how much she likes him, Sita isn't ready to forgive Daz yet. He did run away without her, but he has apologized. More than a few times.

Her glumness over Daz means that today Sita lets me off the hook for being socially inept. Getting off my ass is kinda important today. This morning I had a spectacular wipe-out during practice. Badder than usual. The kind they should give medals for. I went down so hard the other girls stopped their own routines, and Zoë even skated over to make sure I wasn't unconscious. But conking out wasn't my big worry. Because of the way I hit the ice, I have multiple skin abrasions. On my butt. Winnie's worried that I'll fall myself into an avulsion fracture, where basically, it's like a part of your body detaches from the rest. Ga-*ross!* She advised me to warn the school nurse. No way am I letting my teachers or fellow students know that I nearly broke my ass—while figure skating. The first bell rings, and we two glum girls head back inside.

HET-GIRL ALERT: EMBARRASSED THAT HER PEERS MIGHT DISCOVER SHE'S A FIGURE SKATER.

LESBO ALERT: EMBARRASSED THAT HER PEERS MIGHT DISCOVER SHE'S A FIGURE SKATER.

CHAPTER TEN

Every crack of dawn this week, I hurry to practice, skate, dash home, then run to school with my hair sprouting icicles. Every Social Studies class, Max Bledsoe comes up with another way to call me an Ice Princess. "Frost Fairy" is today's moniker.

I've not only crossed him off my kiss-list forever, I'm ready to cross everyone off, girl or boy. Too much cramming takes a ton of energy, especially if you cram for six subjects at once. At practice, Winnie says I look like a decoration on a wedding cake. I'm wobbly on two legs when I should be jack-pine solid on one. Training has kicked in with a vengeance, and it's more than just my legs that ache. I want my parents to be proud of me. I want Sammie to be proud of me, her sister who competes because she loves the game, not the trophy. Ha.

And Sammie. She got sick back in September and took too long to recover. Just the flu, but it hit her hard. She missed a ton of school, and Mom and Dad had to hire a sitter. "I don't need a babysitter!" Sam yelled every morning.

"Oh, hush," was Mom's only reply, though she threw in a little pat on Sam's head. Mom's always sneaking in affection that way, like she doesn't want us to know how much she cares.

Dad's reply was, "Babysitter? Honey, for you we hired a personal jailer." Sammie didn't even pretend to laugh, though she usually cuts Dad some slack when it comes to his gawdawful humour. We both do, cuz we like it that Dad indulges "his girls."

So for weeks Sammie had to stay home from school with a stranger, and she only perked up when either Tyler or I walked through the door, offering to play some serious Funny Bone or Crazy Eights or Mouse Trap—board games and card games, nothing too strenuous. And nothing outdoors. No wonder she's gone stir crazy.

Sammie coughed, and Mom made peppermint tea. Sam wiped sweat from her forehead, and Tyler set up the summer fan. Sita and I put a hold on a lot of stuff, just so I could spend my extra minutes with Sam. But by early October, Sam went back to school. My shoulders feel like they'd been hunched up at my ears for weeks and are finally lowering down to shoulder height.

"It's *Friday*," I announce to Sita when we meet at lunch. "Meet you at your locker before last bell has finished ringing today." After school, we'll head to our coffee shop. Even with a balmy Chinook blowing through the province, I want something hot and sweet to drink. Something with whipped cream. When we get there, Sita treats me to a double with *extra* whipped cream. No Drama Club today, no part-time jobs, no skating practice till tomorrow. Sammie seems all better. Exams may loom, but the Chinook has blown away all our worries. Life is good. Life is grand. Life is—

"So," Sita breaks into my happy thoughts. "You ever going to get a boyfriend or what?" She slurps her mocha and a tuft of whipped cream lands on her chin. Her delicate, cute chin. I can tell about five guys in the place would be willing to lick it off for her.

"Um," is my brilliant reply.

"Oh, for Thor's sake!" Sita says in her best Viking impression. We haven't finished our drinks, but she's signalling that we'll finish them while walking. My heart settles a little lower in my ribcage. The coffee shop—called Lactose Tolerant—is on a slight slope on the crescent above the elementary school we used to go to. This time of day, the playground is teeming with mud rats, and their screams reach in every direction. Most teens avoid the crest, so we're alone. Sita and I walk over to a good-sized boulder wedged between the parking lot of the strip mall and the elementary school fence and lean on it. We can rest our feet against the wire fence and our backs against the boulder, and if we lean way back, we can let our faces absorb the bracing, blue sky. Absolutely *nobody* will interrupt us. I pull my head away from the rock, then lean back again. How to start?

"You like girls, right?" says Sita. "Just straight out admit you're a lesbian, and then we can get past this stupid charade." Her words have cemented my butt to this rock. Does this mean I'm a known lesbian, now? "Tell me the truth, and we'll go back in and order another round." She crumples her cup but keeps it in her hand, waiting for me to concur with her conclusion, dispute her deductions, anything.

What about ... I don't know. In the sky, a band of pure white with scarlet streaks criss-cross above the arch. I know I am avoiding Sita's question. Why? She's given me a way to enter this conversation, but my body refuses to respond. My head stays lolled back, my toes touching the fence. Thirty seconds go by. A minute. Two minutes. Or maybe two hours have passed, I can't tell any more. When I don't answer, Sita gets up and heads back to Lactose Tolerant to flirt with the guy behind the counter. I'm guessing she'll wait for me.

I decide to walk around the boulder once, then go in. I'll follow her and smile at the guy taking orders. I'll reach into my pocket and not only pay but leave a huge tip. I'll slap Sita's elbow and sigh and tell her how glad I am that this pesky secret is out in the open and now we can *really* tell each other our secrets. Except the boulder won't release my hand. I lift one finger off the rock, then the next. I lift my thumb. I can't leave Sita hanging any longer. I realize that it's getting to be that time when we should head home, and that if I don't have this conversation with Sita *now*, I'll have to have it on Monday. At school. Between classes in a crowded hallway or at lunch with Joline and The Two brushing our elbows. Definitely not.

My fingers lift off the cool stone, my feet carry me toward the coffee shop, and my mouth starts to rehearse, saying words like "gay" and "lesbian" and "bisexual" and "experimenting." I still don't know what words I should use to tell my best friend about myself. Which of those words means *me*? I still don't know if declaring that I'm "homosexual" will be an honest confession or just a cop-out. I still don't know. I go into the coffee shop, sit down, and spill.

LESBO ALERT: *TOO SCARED TO TELL HER BEST FRIEND HER INNERMOST DESIRES.*

HET-GIRL ALERT: *TOO SCARED TO TELL HER BEST FRIEND HER INNERMOST DESIRES.*

CHAPTER ELEVEN

Mr Grier says writers should never begin a story with a climactic statement: "The axe hung in the air above her neck!" because, really, there's not much room after the climax for much else except getting your head cut off. The axe comes down on the innocent neck, or some hero saves the day. The End. In other words, after the climax, there's only ever gonna be anti-climax. And usually, the anti-climax sucks.

Maybe I remember his words because Sita's waiting, no matter how long I take to join her. Maybe because the place *is* full, even if our seats are far from everyone except the guy behind the counter. Or maybe because—sex and everything being so complicated—I just have to start at the beginning. The beginning of the beginning. Once I plunk down beside her, I start to describe the bus ride to Nordegg.

But Sita's having none of it. "Please tell me I don't have to hear *more* about forest-fire prevention and proper waste disposal methods. You're getting to the kissing a girl part, right?"

"Not exactly," I reply and receive such a look of disgust I almost make up a sex scene right on the spot. "Look, let's walk, please. Back to our rock?" Sita glares. I hop off my chair and pretend to dust off my brand-new retro jeans.

"Fine." She gracefully untangles her legs from around the chair and leads me out the door. Back at our boulder, I start by telling her about Dianne. "She's older, but not by much—twenty-three—which sounds old, I know, but when I first saw her I thought she was another junior ranger, just like Surge and me."

"I figured you had nothing to kiss out there but skunks and beavers." She has the decency to redden. "I mean *otters*." Sita tucks her hands inside her sweater. Chinook or no Chinook, when the sun disappears on a winter day, it's freezing out. "Your texts were enigmatic sentences about *wildlife*."

And with the sun disappearing, the Chinook warmth will quickly seep away, too. I pick up my storytelling pace. "Dianne had the *cutest* nose, and when she talked, her Aussie vowels hiked all over her tongue." This is what Sita wanted to hear, right? That I don't have a boyfriend because I, duh, like girls? "I cracked up every time she said 'I know' because it sounded like 'Oiy naaaooow.'" I hear my story through Sita's expression; does she want me to get to the kissing part? Or does it bug the hell out of her to hear her best friend finds some girl's nose adorable? Or is my accent just that terrible?

"Okay, it wasn't just her vowels," I add. "She was, I don't know, sexy." When I say that word, I avoid looking at Sita. It's all or nothing right now. But what if Sita blurted out that question because she wants me to deny it? Still, I plunge further into my story. "Dianne treated us like we were as grownup as she was. Or like she was still a teenager like us."

"Grownups get in trouble if they kiss teenagers." Sita doesn't even sound sarcastic when she says that, just worried. She's leaning back against the rock, huddled against the now-cool winds. Maybe huddled against where my story's going?

"No, wait—listen." I explain that Dianne had an awesome dyke hairdo, wore the most adorable ranger shorts ever, never wore lipstick, and smiled at me way more than she did at Surge. "And Dianne also only had till the end of summer, same as me. She could only work in Canada for a year, on exchange. Come the end of September, she was going back to Perth."

Go on, finish the story, Sita's hand wave implores me. I take a *huge* breath. All or nothing.

"Okay, so I figured she might kiss me if she knew I liked her, since we both were going to be on opposite ends of the globe pretty soon."

Sita squishes her paper cup, and actually tosses it into a regular garbage bin. Uh-oh! I grab my heart back from the tip of one of the mountains on the horizon and stuff it fast inside my jacket. "Then, suddenly, it's our last day. It was now or never, I thought, if anything could happen with Dianne."

"Let me guess," says Sita. "You're going to gross me out telling me all about kissing someone who's, like, practically a *teacher?*"

"No," I admit. "I didn't kiss her. I wanted to. But I ended up kissing Surge instead. I didn't mean to. I mean, I was going to ask him about what he thought about Dianne." And maybe Surge saw me looking at him. Maybe—like me—he just figured that day was the last one we had left.

We'd been walking around, I tell Sita, and I thought he'd been quite a few feet to my left. I hadn't thought, because without coming any closer, he was holding my hips, pressing his vanilla lips against my neck. And, in spite of my total shock—a boy is trying to kiss me! a boy is kissing me!—I leaned down, my lips parted and softened, and—

"And? And?!" For once, I'm the one with details and Sita's the one whose job it is to pry those details out of me.

"And we kissed. And kept kissing. And walking. Except we had to stop doing the one to do the other." The boulder's exterior feels rough against my shoulders, comfortably bumpy and coarse. "We tried walking *and* kissing, but I tripped. So we mostly held hands, with about seventy-five kissing breaks before we got back to the main office." I should have told Sita this story before. She's jumping up slightly onto her toes (though that may have been from the chill), and clapping her hands (again, might have been—).

"You kissed a boy? You really kissed a boy!" She sounds so excited and happy for me, I don't need to jump around to keep warm. "So you *don't* like girls? You're normal, right? Except, like, maybe just a late bloomer?"

I shouldn't have told Sita this story. Or told it in a different way. Her response is exactly why I haven't said anything before today. My heart goes from racing along the skyline with the Chinook winds to thudding against the backdrop of the mountains. I could just say to her: yes, I like boys. It would be true. And Sita and I would be back to our usual rapport. Except *she's* the one who tried to boot me out of my miniscule closet-box, and now I'm just gonna let her cram me back in? Where's that explanatory nametag when I need it?

"It was just kissing," I tell her. "Surge was—"

"Wow," Sita exhales this word. Finally, something about my Smokey-the-Bear summer is worth listening to.

"I really liked kissing Surge, Sita," I tell her. "I really did." Sita nods encouragingly. "But I was kinda sad too, because I was also thinking about what it would have been like to kiss Dianne." Yes, truth be true, *while* he was kissing me. "And I knew that I'd never get a chance to kiss her, and maybe not kiss any girl, if some boy has his tongue down my throat."

Maybe I shouldn't be so crude. Maybe I should try to make day-dreaming about a girl a bit more, well, daydreamy. But if Sita is going to be mad at me, it may as well be for the whole hog, the stuffed swine, the full-blown boar.

After years and years of not telling my best friend about my kiss-ing wishes, I now wish to tell Sita absolutely everything. I've been in one box for too long. And not just the either/or, but the in-between, too. All or ...

"... nothing! Absolutely nothing would make me kiss a girl." She folds her arms in front of her chest, as if protecting her breasts from me.

Yipes, is Sita getting nervous that my confession puts her in dan-ger of unwanted lust from me? "Sita, you don't think that I like *you?*" I think how to best reassure her. "I would never—I mean, you're my friend, I don't want ... "

"Look, K," Sita pouts. "Do you really ever think about kissing *me?* Do you? *Fuck a duck!*" As if kissing hypothetical Dianne is okay, as long as there's a Surge in the punchline. As long as Sita doesn't have to feel a lesbo-kiss on her own lips.

My face gets very red then and my hands start to sweat, even though I took my mitts off at lunch and forgot them in my locker. "Fuck a duck," for some reason, sounds so mean.

"NO!" I yell at her. I yell it so loud everyone back in the coffee shop can hear me. So loud that all the birds left in the city rise up as one and choose migration that very second. "You don't even ... *No!*"

"Stop yelling!" she yells. "Do you think I'm like you?" she whispers angrily, even though no one else is around. "You think *I* should be kissing girls?" Oh no. All I need to do is say something. Anything. My brain begs my mouth to glide.

Instead, my legs pay heed. I push off from the rock and I run.

This little queer girl runs alllllll the way home.

IDJIT ALERT: *SHE FINALLY CONFESSES HER DEEP, SECRET SELF TO HER BEST FRIEND, AND THEN BLOWS THE LANDING.*

CHAPTER TWELVE

What I'd heard Sita say was, "Do you want to kiss *me?*" but maybe she said, "*Do* you want to kiss me?" I don't know what I was thinking, telling my boy-crazy best friend that I (sometimes) like girls.

The closet may be cramped, but it's not like anyone else is scrunched in here with me. At nearly sixteen, I haven't done more than kiss, so I can last a few more years without confession, yes? Once Sita reaches university, she'll hang out with loads of gay drama boys and funky lez-chique girls, and my problems will seem laughable. Then, when I'm legal, I'll head to some big, bad lezzie bar downtown. By telling Sita now, I've forced myself into a very lonely high school box. No lunch buddy (yeah, like Amanda or Joline will stay loyal to a freak), no in-between-classes waves, no Friday afternoon dates. Uh-oh, maybe the fact that I call them "dates" is also freaking Sita out. Maybe she thinks that I think ...

No phone call from Sita during dinner, which she knows drives my mom batty, but which she also knows is the best time to catch me in a semi-static state. For once, I don't scarf down everything in sight, but Mom doesn't notice my uneaten food at the end of the meal. Even Sammie's distracted by the Explorer Passport she made in art class, with a page for every campground we'll visit next summer. I start to clear the table without being asked, in case I need to deke out for a quick meet-n-greet with Sita before bedtime. Nada. And no text messages on Saturday. Or Sunday.

I absolutely, truly, ridiculously miss texting with Sita. Back in the summer, she may not have wanted to hear much news about a herd of bison that broke through a containment fence, or the highest fire hazard warning in eleven years, but she was excellent at sending me juicy zingers: "True story: Talia Sitkins went on a date with a cop and she's only fifteen! Her parents grounded her and his boss grounded him!" And: "Sliced my index finger helping my dad cook elaborate lamb and chickpea meal. Hospital and seven stitches. Here's a pic of the wound before repair. Here's an after pic." Loved the news and was *très* grateful that my phone couldn't handle photos! And: "When, when, when r u back? Calgary is dull. I am dull. Save me before I befriend Talia Sitkins! that is how desperate I am ..." You gotta love a friend who lets you know you're missed!

Goes without saying that my phone's on permanent silent mode, so it never rings, beeps, or in any way tells me I've got mail. Doesn't matter: I check my messages every 4.6 seconds at home. All I need is a buffer like a sweater or a dinner napkin or the couch, and the parents don't notice me punch in the letters. It's beautiful. Of course, I can't ever call people back, so my friends have to accept the "I don't really have a cellphone, but I'll text you anyway" sitch. Luckily, most kids my age don't do much with their phones besides text. But Surge kept *calling*.

That first week, I barely missed him, though that may have been cuz I'd barely thought about him in any way before the kiss. Was Surge my boyfriend? I didn't know, and I sure wasn't going to ask him. Eventually, I'd ask Sita. And once I told her about this new boy in my life, she'd use her wisdom gained from listening in on her sisters' phone calls to steer me in the right direction.

Except, there was that part of me that knew (feared?) just how happy she'd be about this boyfriend business. So for weeks I let Sita talk about Luscious Lucien and Tony Baloney and Dreamy Daz. I kept Surge as a party surprise, there to bring out whenever I needed to establish my true het-girl-ness. Except that plan really backfired. Mega-failure.

Sita's the one who tells *me* that I like girls, and I bring the Surge story out as *proof* of my girl-attraction? And then I go and get mad at her for not understanding stuff that I don't even have the first clue about?

HET-GIRL ALERT: *MISSES TEXTING WITH THE BOY, EVEN THOUGH THEY HAVEN'T EXACTLY WRITTEN TO EACH OTHER A LOT.*

LESBO ALERT: *NOTICES THAT SHE DOESN'T HAVE A LOT TO SAY TO THE BOY, AND FEARS YUMMY KISSING IS NOT ENOUGH.*

IDJIT ALERT: *THINKS THAT NOT BEING FULLY ENAMOURED WITH HER BOYFRIEND (BOYFRIEND? I HAVE A BOYFRIEND?) MEANS SHE MIGHT BE A LESBIAN.*

CHAPTER THIRTEEN

Mom does this thing right at the beginning and end of every yoga workout. Her yoga guru teaches that people matter to other people, even when we haven't all met each other. I don't get how twisting your foot over your head is the path toward Peace on Earth, but Mom eats this stuff up. She even does hand actions to accompany the words.

Hands to forehead: "passionate thought." Hands to mouth: "passionate speech." Hands to chest: "passionate heart." Mom recites this chant for weeks. Sometimes when she gets home from work, sometimes in the evening when Dad's at work. And sometimes on the weekends just before I fly off to skating practice. I think of telling Winnie about the chant, but she's not a hippie type. Then again, neither is my mom. Or she didn't used to be, anyway. Who knew Mom had passion anywhere, let alone in her heart?

For one minute, for sixty desperate seconds, I consider telling Mom about my falling out with Sita. I walk in the door expecting a lecture about how Mom's sick of me being late for every Friday supper. Again. Instead, she's pushed aside the coffee table covered with Sammie's 1,000-piece snowflake puzzle and is down on her mat, deep into—you guessed it—the Plow pose. I stand in the hall, wondering if I should interrupt. Then I hear the chant.

Hands to forehead: "compassionate thought." Hands to mouth: "compassionate speech." Hands to chest: "compassionate heart." COMpassionate. She's not celebrating *passion*, the chant's all about respecting the masses out there. Funny how empathy never begins at home. If I tell her Sita and I had a big blow-out, she'll only say that Sita and I are going through a rough patch. And I'm certainly not ready to tell her a blow-out about *what*. So I skip the heart-to-heart, set the table in dead silence, listen to Sam describe the stamps she'll create for future campground passports, and go to sleep mad. And sad and empty and lonely. Only Sita would understand how I feel.

My parents married young, real young, like, right-out-of-high-school young. You think having "youthful" parents is a good thing? Let me correct you on that one: I had to bargain like crazy to get my parents to allow me to work part-time—like being a teenager and wanting cash is a sin. For my parents, it's practically a felony. They don't want me getting stuck in what they call a dead-end job.

That's how my *mother* thinks, anyway, about being "just" a secretary. She's senior secretary at an insurance firm, so she has to be there before everyone else, make sure the boardrooms are set up, new flowers have been ordered, that the appointments book is updated, blah, blah, blah. I can see why she's bored, but instead of trying to get me to university, why doesn't she just go back to school herself?

My dad *likes* his job. Right after their honeymoon, Dad took a bartending course and had no problem finding part-time work right away. A couple of years after they married, he got a full-time bartending position at a skanky bar downtown. Since then, he's worked his way up to a swanky hotel. "Oil execs or party boys, come the end of the day, they all want to wet their whistle." Means he works late, works every weekend, but he gets paid well, *and* gets pretty amazing tips.

Mom thinks being a secretary and bartender isn't swank enough. But why does she care? It's not like she's into fancy clothes or gadgets or going out a lot. I get that kids cost a lot, especially extras like Sammie's bath supports or my competition fees. But she's always telling Dad that he should take a course, upgrade. What's he supposed to do, only serve champagne and not beer?

We usually go through our Sunday morning chores silently, but I've barely spoken to anyone in my family since Friday.

"So how come secretary school was good enough for *you?*" I demand of Mom. Not fair, as she's pretty sensitive about not having gotten a "higher" education. I'm so sick of being on the rotten end of fights. And always losing. I guess I'm picking a fight because I'm so mad that Sita's abandoned me. Mom should treat me like I know what I'm doing with my life. Even if I asked nicely about her hopes and dreams, she wouldn't talk to me like I'm a person, only a daughter. When we do talk, she usually gives me a lecture about the opportunities I'll get from a solid education: the chances to see other parts of the world and how I should not just think about a job, but plan for a career, etc. But this time, she just answers my question. Sort of.

"Maybe it *wasn't* good enough for me," she replies, quite softly.

I groan because she's trying to manipulate me through pity. She puts a finger to her lips. We have to be quiet while cleaning the house because of Dad's late shift. I should tell her about Sita. Some of it. But I'm just too weary for a lecture right now. And if we wake Dad, he'll be grumpy all day.

Sunday mornings I scrub the kitchen floor, dust the living room, and straighten my and Sam's bedroom. Actually, Sam's supposed to straighten our room, but I usually sneak in and pick up anything from the floor, so all Sam has to do is roll around shoving jeans and T-shirts into waist-high drawers. She's not a total slob, but she does amass loads of books and crayons and bungee cords. Mom also makes me wash all the dishes that have piled up over the weekend. Why can't we get a dishwasher?

This afternoon, I have skating practice. And the whole family will share a meal tonight, even Tyler, because Sunday evening is the only day and time nobody works or has try-outs or football practice or fund-raising events or a game. Or friends, apparently.

Tyler doesn't have to wash dishes or clean under furniture. Come noon, he vacuums the carpets, plus his bedroom and my parents.' Then he's free.

Sam has to clean the bathroom sink and change the towels.

Last night, Dad's shift ended at four in the morning. Mom explains that the volleyball team from the University of Calgary came in to celebrate a win and stayed way past last-call. Dad's been on this topsy-turvy schedule since I was a kid. Which means we all have to tip-toe around most mornings, but it also means he's usually out later than anyone in the world, so he isn't the one enforcing my strict curfew.

By next semester, Tyler will have bags full of sports scholarships, if he doesn't already.

Thing is, there's no point in crying "unfair" to parents. I learned that when Tyler not only stole my purple flying dinosaur but dissected it. When I "dissected" his soccer shirt in retaliation, he didn't even cry, just handed the shredded jersey to Mom.

"Clothes are not toys, Keira," she told me when I explained about my stuffed animal. "Tyler's punishment is losing those toys, too."

"But he wrecked my slinky *and* my dinosaur—it's not fair," I wailed.

"No, life isn't very often fair," she answered. How's that for comforting a five-year-old? Tyler's had it easy ever since. He knows he won't get shite for doing shite. But I have learned to adapt. I have learned to manipulate the manipulators. Since life ain't fair, you have to be sharp. You have to listen to parents. I don't mean *obey* them, I mean listen to the kind of language they use against you. Words are their tools, but you can steal them and use them for good instead of evil.

LESBO ALERT: MOURNS MORE FOR THE LOSS OF HER GIRL FRIENDSHIP THAN WHATEVER IT WAS SHE HAD WITH THE BOY.

HET-GIRL ALERT: MOURNS MORE FOR THE LOSS OF HER GIRL FRIENDSHIP THAN WHATEVER IT WAS SHE HAD WITH THE BOY.

CHAPTER FOURTEEN

You'd think kissing a boy, possibly having a boyfriend, and telling your best friend about girl-boy details wouldn't lead to a total breakdown of the friendship, would you? Wrong. Today's Thursday. Sita and I have now gone almost a week with no phone calls, no texts, not a single lunch together.

All week I ate alone. I spent English class alone. I trudged home alone. The only time I saw Sita outside class was yesterday by the lockers. She was about to head off to Drama Club, and I thought that maybe I could walk her to the theatre room. I started toward her locker, but she slammed it shut to head off in the opposite direction. Right at the same time, Jason Billings was passing by and called her a "slut" right to her back (brave boy). Her shoulders slumped. This was my cue.

Except this time, I kept my mouth shut. My stomach crawled with baby snakes for not defending Sita, but instead of saying anything, instead of running to catch up with Sita, I just let Jason get away with being the kind of creep he'll always be. When he walked by me, he smirked and gave me the finger.

Today, Rumpled takes our class to the library for a Research day, which means that besides the teacher, we also have a librarian hovering around. Instead of rows of desks, we sit in groups at round tables. We're supposed to compare research methods, so we're allowed to quietly chat.

I arrive first, and grab a table by the doors as Sita sits at the table farthest from me that she can find. She's in the Arctic and I'm in Mexico. Or the other way around. I'm not sure who's the most frozen these days.

My table starts chatting about how we get Monday off for Thanksgiving, then how soon the first dance is coming up at the end of the month. Since Hallowe'en falls on a Friday this year, we're pretty hyped.

"You're going solo, right, Keira?" Amanda asks, waving her pencil case in my face. So she's noticed that lately Sita and I haven't been sewn together at the hip.

"Yeah, we could walk there together," I answer.

"Um, no, I'm going with Titus," Amanda replies. "We hooked up at last week's kegger. You weren't there, were you?" Guess she was oh-so-deliberately *not* handing me an invite. My turn to feel like the idjit third wheel. After that, I actually spend library time doing research for my term paper.

Then Jason creeps into the library—either he has a free period, or he's skipping what he refers to as "Physics for Phags"—and whisper-yells, "Keira's a big fat lezbo!" Which is kind of ridic, given that, if anything, I'm an ultra-skinny lesbian.

Everybody's heads slowly swivel towards me. The worst part is, I'm sure my sarcastic thought about me being too skinny to be a *fat* lesbian is exactly what Sita's thinking, but she doesn't say a thing.

Max Bledsoe is the one who stands up in my defence. "Look, man, on behalf of my cousin the art-fag, it's an insult for you to go around complimenting undeserving girls by calling them lesbians. Lay off the straight girls and pick on some of your own brethren, okay?"

Yep, he saves my Ice Princess ass with his class-clownery. Everyone applauds, and Jason gets a look on his face like he's figuring out that Max's comment just might be a dig about *him* being gay. Then Mr Rempel pokes his head around the encyclopaedia stacks and says, "Back to work, people!"

People! Like teenagers are a separate species, or something.

❆

Winnie calls in the morning about an ice rink cancellation and tells me to get my butt down to the community rink on Friday after school. No biggie, I have nothing to do then, anyway. When Sam hears this, she invents a sob story for her bus driver so that he'll drop her off at the rink and she can watch my new routine. (She told him that our mom volunteers at the bingo hall inside the community centre to raise money for kids like her who don't even *have* a mom. That kid is going to make an amazing politician some day: she can talk anyone into anything. Except our parents.)

"Your routine is HEX-cellent, Keira!" she shouts to me when I emerge from the change room. "I like the part where your bum kissed the ice. Twice!" She's pretty pleased with herself that she's managed a rhyme about me falling.

"Yeah, well, I'm still working out the kinks." I shove my skates and mega-tonnage of books into the netting that swings under Sam's seat, then tug open the arena doors so she can zip through them.

"Bobby Robbie at school says ice skating is for bent boys or kinky kids. Is that true?"

Her question sets off the live snakes inside my belly. How early do kids start learning these kinds of insults? "His words or yours?" I ask.

"Bobby Robbie says 'bent' means the same as 'queer,' and I like what you do when words all start with the same letter, you know, bent b—"

"His name is really Bobby Robbie?" That stops her. Sam's thinking now. And I can tell she was also expecting a lecture about how it's not nice to call names, yada yada.

"Teacher calls him Bobby Robbie," which, for anyone Sam's age, is pretty good proof that it must be her classmate's real name, cuz, like, a grownup would never make fun of other people, right?

"And your friend knows all about stuff like this?"

"We're not friends." Sam is definite in her dismissal of that possibility. "Bobby Robbie says his older brother did ice skating when he was little but their mom made him stop because if his brother had kept skating he'd be bent—and bent and queer and kinky all mean you're going to hell." Sam sometimes doesn't even breathe when she talks; it just all comes out like one long, extended phrase.

Sam doesn't really know why this kid's mother yanked his brother out of skating. She doesn't know what queer or kinky mean or how they're being used by her classmates. She's a good kid, and I don't want to lecture her. But I've done enough not speaking up this week and for my entire life. Even if Sam doesn't know these words, she'll get to know them. The last thing I could stand is if my beloved baby sister some day hurled the lesbo insult at me. At anyone.

"Hey, lots of boys are bent, you know."

"Like that tree?" She points at a tree split in two, with half its trunk growing along the ground. We're at the curb waiting for the light to change. Sam reaches out her hand, cuz she's not allowed to cross streets by herself.

"Sorta like that tree. But also not like that tree." I take a deep breath. "Sometimes boys who like boys get called names. Like bent. Or fag. Mean names, you know?"

"Yeah, like Bobby Robbie calls me 'spaz' sometimes."

At that, I have to keep my hands from forming fists and punching the poor tree. I keep forgetting what Sam has to put up with from other kids, from random grownups, even from teachers, sometimes.

"Tyler and his friends mostly like boys. Does that mean they're all bent?" she asks.

I can't help it, I burst out laughing. I so, soooooo want to tell my sister that, yes, Tyler and his friends are all bent boys. But I'm on a mission here.

"Maybe some of them. But people usually call a boy 'bent' when he wants to *be with* another boy, like Tyler dating a girlfriend. But it's not just boys who date girls. Some girls go out with girls, and some boys go out with boys. You with me?"

"Tyler says he doesn't like to be in a shack with a girlfriend, but to date lots and lots of different fan-girls," Sam explains.

Right. "Okay, but I'm just saying that liking boys or liking girls has nothing to do with skating or football or anything else you do, okay?"

"Okay-doe-KAY." Sam's done with this convo, so she zips ahead, rolling down the hill faster than I want to run. No wonder Mom worries she could topple over and crack a bone some day.

Once we're home, Sam and I hustle to get inside before Mom finds out about the extra outing. "But you're still Da Kinky Kid, right?" Sam throws her jacket on the floor as she enters. For me to pick up before Mom sees.

Which is in about two minutes. We hear Mom enter through the back door, saying, "We're celebrating Thanksgiving on Sunday this year; your dad's hotel bar is catering a private gig on Monday afternoon." No, "Hey, Keira, I notice you're home early these days, is everything all right?" Not that I'd tell her, but you'd think she'd notice this is the second Friday that I'm not squeaking through the door twenty-nine seconds before supper.

"Yay, turkey!" Sam chimes in. I don't blame her. We love a good turkey feast in our house, but Thanksgiving and New Year's are the only two times a year we get to indulge.

"Don't talk with your mouth full, honey." Mom gives Sam that "you're-not-a-baby-any more" look. Which is a total hypocrite move, because she expects Sam to act like some sort of nineteenth-century grownup lady, but then treats her like she wouldn't wipe her own nose after sneezing.

"It's gum," I throw in. "You have to be able to talk when you're chewing gum or you never get to say anything." I grab my skates out of Sam's chair, making sure Mom doesn't notice, and head to the bathroom to hang them up. "Meet you at the coffee table, Sam."

Mom is never wrong. "Well, then, I guess we weigh our choices: double-mint chew or voicing our opinions," she says to both of us.

Dad never rags on us like this about pointless rules. Her lecture continues: "And make sure there's no mud on those wheels."

Sometimes I think Mom would make Sammie leave her wheelchair outside the front door, just to make her own life neater. But at least she doesn't stop Sam from having some fun with me. For over an hour, Sammie and I play the Loco Licorice board game. Every time she lands in the Dumpling Dungeon, Sam blows a bubble.

"How much gum you got in there?" I ask, popping the monster boil so it's all over her face.

"Hmmfre spuutskav blreisce," she answers, shoving bits of bubble back into her mouth. Just our rotten luck: Mom sticks her head into the room at that exact moment.

"Sammie. Gum. Garbage." Like she doesn't even need verbs any more. Sam wheels toward the kitchen, and Mom adds: "Bathroom. Hands. And face." I pick up the dice, ready for my turn. Mom knows I probably popped that bubble, but she doesn't make me go wash my hands like a baby. "And Keira," Mom starts, and waits for me to turn around and face her. I carefully set the dice back onto the board with a six and six facing up, to see if Sam will fall for my trick.

"What?" I ask. Not too polite, yeah, but Fridays are my time. Even if Mom hasn't noticed that Sita and I are on a friendship hiatus, she should respect the one post-school afternoon I get for myself.

"What do you think if this Thanksgiving we have lasagne instead of turkey?"

Is she kidding? "No way!" I almost upset the board by slapping my palm down hard. "We only get turkey twice a year. Sam *loves* turkey!" I love turkey, Tyler loves turkey. "C'mon, Mom, Dad loves carving the turkey. He, like, gets off on being the provider-guy or something." She doesn't care what her kids want, but maybe she'll cave for her own husband?

"Look," Mom comes closer and actually lowers her voice. "This year money is a bit tight." Her mouth stretches like she's smiling and angry at the same time. "Your dad and I are trying to cut corners where we can. If lasagne doesn't work for you, then how about—"

"No way, Mom. No—absolute—way." I lower my voice too. "Okay, look, I get that you have to guard the dimes, I do, but... " And I stop there, because how can you argue when a parent tells you they haven't figured out how to be smart with money?

"Keira, honey, don't fret." Mom pats my arm, like I'm too young to deal with big grownup issues like providing supper for your family. That does it.

"I'll buy the turkey," I blurt out.

Her hand snaps away like my sweater's bitten her. "That's not the—"

"Yes, it *is* the point. I have a job now. I can afford one lousy Thanksgiving meal. And I have a bank account."

"You are *not* taking money out of the bank. Not for any reason. Certainly not for *this* reason!" And she actually stamps her foot. I almost laugh, but I'm not suicidal.

"I'm trying to help out, Mom."

We both hear Sammie flush, and we both—instant presto—calm down.

"As a matter of fact, I *do* need you to do some shopping for me, thanks for asking," Mom says, just as Sam wheels back into the room.

Who knew my mother could be an expert at devious? "I'll get the list, and here's fifty dollars." She doesn't even have the decency to be embarrassed that she's had the money all along. "If you come across a turkey smaller than ten pounds in the frozen meats, buy it and we'll defrost it in the sink tonight and tomorrow."

"I get to go! I get to go!" Sammie yells. Not knowing there's been an argument brewing. Not knowing what the stakes are. I'm not so sure what the stakes are, either. If money isn't the point, then *what*?

"A' course you can come along, Sam," I say before Mom can get in a word. Sam whooshes over to the front door to gather her coat and mitts.

Mom and I are both a little pissed off but playing nice in front of Sam. Which is pretty weird, as Mom is one of those parents who doesn't do pretend nice. Not in front of her kids, anyway.

So, basically, life sucks right now: Mom wants to skimp on Thanksgiving dinner, I don't think I have a boyfriend any more (Surge's texts have stopped, probably cuz I've stopped, too), no girl-friend in sight, and now I don't even have my best friend. That leaves Sam, and it's a good thing we make a team against the rest of the world.

You know what's wrong with the world? *People*, that's what! There I am with Sammie, picking up a frozen turkey, a giant bag of rice, and celery for Thanksgiving stuffing. Sam's having a ball because the week-long Chinook has not only melted all the snow, but the cool nights have refrozen the melts into clumps of porous moon debris that she's trying to roll over with her wheelchair. We're half-way through the parking lot, headed for the Dairy Bar—which

I admit is totally ridic in winter, but Sam absolutely adores their hot chocolate. My clunky boots skitter all over the ice, but Sam's motorized wheelchair can practically scale mountains. She keeps hooting every time my feet splay, so I just finally drop myself onto her lap.

"Drive, minion!" I command, and we chariot it through the rest of the parking lot.

And then some jerk leaning out of his four-wheel-drive truck yells at us. "This ain't the Special Olympics!" he snarls.

"Yeah, well, getting into the Olympics is *hard*," I yell back. Not the best rejoinder, but double stars to me for saying something out loud.

I hop off the wheelchair at the entrance to the Dairy Bar, Sam slaps at the blue oversized button, and the door slides open. "Hot cocoa, ready or not!" I turn to see if that jerk made her lose her appetite.

"Ready!" she calls back. Not much can make the girls in my family lose our appetites.

IDJIT ALERT: SADLY, THEY BLARE OUT ALL TOO OFTEN ...

CHAPTER FIFTEEN

Tonight, after our Thanksgiving dinner—*with* turkey, thank you very much—Sam and I clear away and do the dishes.

"Why are you mad at Sita?" Sam asks, handing me the ugly green glass salad bowl.

"I'm not mad at Sita." I shove the bowl behind the camping mugs and plastic yogurt containers.

Sam snorts. "Then how come she wasn't here for supper?" Good point. When our families celebrate holidays on different days (or different holidays), we usually eat at each other's house. Sita and I haven't talked in over a week, now. Nine-and-a-half days.

"The times they are a-changing, little sister." I fold leftover turkey into aluminum foil and shove it in the fridge. Turkey sandwiches for a week. I'm not complaining.

Another snort. "Why are you mad at Sita?" she asks again.

"I'm not mad at Sita. We're just not good friends any more." Sorta true. It's not that I want to lie to Sam, I just don't quite have a story that makes sense. Not even to me.

"How come?"

Yeah, how come? How to tell my baby sister that I like girls and because I do, my best girlfriend doesn't like me any more? Or because I like girls, it freaks her out that I might like her or expect her to join the lesbo club. Or something. I'm actually a bit confused about why Sita and I are fighting. Or even *if* we're fighting. I hope we're fighting, cuz that means we can make up. Right now, we're just not being friends. Which sucks.

"Don't be silly," I say instead. "I see her every day at school." Lying is so easy when you do it by telling the truth. "After we're done here, you wanna digest our delicious dinner with a round of Cheat?"

I grab an extra towel and help with the drying. So we finish the dishes, Sam rounds up Tyler and Dad (Mom's in her bedroom working out next week's family schedule), and everybody cheats and cheats and cheats, and Sammie wins the game. The whole time, I don't think about Sita or Surge or Dianne or anybody. Till I'm alone in my bed.

I haven't texted Surge in ages. We don't have much to share, except different versions of *goodbye* and *I miss you*. I saved him up so I'd have a *wow* of a story to hand over to Sita—"Oh, didn't I mention I have a boyfriend?"—but I waited too long. By the time I got around to telling her, I didn't actually have that boyfriend any more.

Lying in bed, digesting what has turned out to be the most cal-orified Thanksgiving dinner ever (we not only had turkey, but Dad brought home a double-layer ice-cream cake for dessert), I taste vanilla when I lick my lips.

Have I mentioned that kissing Surge made me squirm? In a good way, obviously, but also in a totally *I'm-freaking-out-here* way. All I've wanted for the past few years is to shed my ultra-virgin status and at least kiss someone. I've been openly lusting after boys with Sita, and secretly lusting after girls with my pillow. I thought that if I just kissed someone—boy or girl—I'd find out who I am. Surge was the test case, right? I wanted to throw him on the grass and press my lips into his until we flew up into the night sky and became the Gemini constellation, our mouths melded, our hands forever clasping. But I also wanted to jump up and run away and hide in my dorm till after the north-bound bus left the next morning.

Which is why I need to talk to Sita right now. She'd explain away my confusion. She'd help me figure me out. In a way, maybe she already has.

I pull out my phone from inside my slipper and text Surge: "mis yr smyl, yr laf, yr smyl." Surge wasn't texting his friends all summer, like I thought, but playing war games on his phone. He's not so great with words. Now that I've written to him once again, maybe he'll get enthusiastic in return? Except, once he reads my message, he'll probably try to call me. And when I don't answer, we'll go back to blank-blank-blank. I fall asleep sad. I'm so tired of not having anyone to talk to!

✳

Next day at lunch, Joline's eating a chorizo-with-anise sandwich. She waves it under my nose.

"Take a bite, I dare you." Joline tries to get her sandwich close enough to my face to scrape against my skin.

"You know anise only smells like licorice," I inform her. "What are you, in grade two?"

"Is that supposed to be an insult? Isn't your sister seven years old? Are you trying to insult *me* by comparing me to *your sister*?" I swipe away the sandwich and it slides across the table. Joline just grabs it and keeps munching. She thinks she can make anyone do what she wants: even get me to eat something that smells like licorice. Maybe a mild skin rash will at least get me out of English class?

Twenty times this week, I've started to text Sita about what a humongous pain Joline is, but I stop my fingers before hitting "send." I'm the one who confessed. And then, yes, we both behaved in un-best-friend ways by not defending the other.

My phone stays blank all week. No texts from Sita and none from Surge. My first whirlwind romance: two days of smooching plus a downward slope of dwindling texting.

When I was twelve, Sita's family took me to Banff for a long weekend (no exams in sight, and all assignments already handed in). All the sisters came, even Amila and Valia, who'd both moved to Vancouver but flew back just to cram into a car with parents and siblings (and one sibling friend) in the middle of February. Skiing that powdered snow felt like skating an avalanche. Sita and I twirled and swirled past the bendy poles and pristine moguls like our home had always been these slopes. For two days. On the third morning, I got up too early and went for a skate while everyone else slept. By breakfast, I'd improved my double Loop jump even though the only rink around was a rinky-dink outdoor one. Sita's family couldn't get me to ski at all that final day. I was done.

And now, it seems, Surge is done with me. "Sounds like you miss his lips more than you miss him," I can hear Sita say in my head. Even when she's not here, she's here. The thing is, I want to tell Sita, kissing Surge didn't make me want to kiss boys more or make me want to kiss girls less. I adored kissing him, but those kisses didn't solve all my problems. I just get to be more confused.

And I get to be confused without my best friend helping me sort things out. Or at least offering sarcastic snippets as I'm muddling through the sorting.

IDJIT ALERT: TEEN ALIENATES ALMOST EVERYONE SHE CARES FOR ENTIRELY BECAUSE SHE ACTS OUT OF FEAR THAT SHE MIGHT ALIENATE ABSOLUTELY EVERYONE SHE CARES FOR!

CHAPTER SIXTEEN

Some girl I don't recognize is goofing around with Sam when I get home on the Wednesday after Thanksgiving. Without Sita to walk with, I'm home in record time. And then I see this stranger sitting on our front porch, on this luscious Chinook afternoon, jacket slung over her arm, telling jokes to Sam.

"Knock-knock."

"Who's there?

"Delay."

"Delay who?"

"Adelay-de-hoo!"

"Knock-knock."

"Who's there?

"Socks."

"Socks who?"

"Socks to be you!"

"Knock-knock."

"Who's there?"

"A monster."

"A monster who?"

"Quick! Run for your life!"

Most of the jokes aren't even funny. Most don't even make sense. But Sammie loves jokes that don't make sense. Who is this girl who can make Sam so happy?

Sammie tells me that her school bus blew a cap or something, and the driver commandeered some high school buses to take a few extra elementary kids each. The driver of this one tried to take Sam right to our house, but the bus couldn't get a good enough grip to stop on the hill, so had to go around the corner before stopping. The driver wouldn't let her get off by herself when he couldn't watch her go straight to our house. And he wouldn't leave the rest of the kids alone on the bus. They might have been there for hours had this high school girl not stepped up and said they were close to her stop anyway and she'd walk Sammie to the house.

Sam introduces me, the way she usually does: "This is my sister, Keira, and she's an Ice Capades star." I bow because, really, what else are you going to do with an intro like that?

"And this is Jaaaaaaaaye."

"Jay?" I'm not sure why Sam's drawing out the name, trying to figure out what it is she wants me to pay attention to.

Sammie doesn't let me swing in the wind for long. "No, *Jane*," she corrects me, "but with a 'y'—you know, Jaaaaaaaaayne."

I don't know, but I can see Sammie wants me to somehow pronounce it with the correct spelling. I stick out my hand. "Jaynee? Nice to meet you." My hand hangs around in the air on its own for a while before she takes it.

Her smile is kinda cheerful and sad at the same time. "That's what my brother calls me, too. He'll be here soon," she says, as if I'd asked how long she was going to litter our front porch with her butt.

"You said you lived near this stop," Sammie pipes up, accusingly. Nothing gets by that kid, I tell you.

"Yeah?" Jayne asks. "Are you sure?" And when Sam nods, Jayne slowly crosses her arms over her chest and squishes her lips to the left side of her face. "Guess I *lied* then," she says, as if she herself is just working out the details. "Guess I had my suspicions that there was another person out there in the universe who couldn't get enough knock-knock jokes, so I lied to escape the travelling orange prison." She purses her lips and curves them to the right side of her face.

"Oh my god, those were *jokes?* You were trying to be *funny?*" Sam slaps a palm against her wheelchair like the armrest is a substitute forehead, and she's in the sad position of breaking the news to poor Jayne that her sense of humour is beneath even a seven-year-old.

At that, the sadness falls away, leaving only the cheerful part of Jayne's smile, and she sits back down on the cold cement again. "So, I can wait for my brother to pick me up, even though he has to come from way waaaaaay across town?" She's facing Sam, but I get the feeling her words are aimed at me. She's not wearing makeup, and her hair is pulled back into a ponytail. *Plain Jane*, I think.

"No problemo," I tell her. "Does he really have to come far? Doesn't your school have more buses?" Her smile shoots down a few octaves again.

"I go to Backstrom," she says as if only to Sam, "same as you. We don't have any classes together, but I sat behind you at the first week's assembly. Your sweater dropped off the chair, and I handed it back to you. You said I was your hero."

Her words make a light dance on my spine, although I barely

remember that; I mean, I don't remember *her*, but she remembers *me*. There I was, a newbie to high school, feeling pretty invisible, but she saw me.

"What time do you have lunch period?" I ask, and from her Chinook smile I know I've landed this jump on just the right edge of my blade: clean and still moving. Maybe we can sit together? Maybe her friends can join my friends (if you can count Joline in that category), and soon we'll be a big pack of kids who rule grade ten and …

And then her brother drives up in a Trans Am (I swear) wearing a muscle shirt and backward baseball cap. It's not that warm any more, but he doesn't have any kind of winter gear on and even has the window rolled down with a bare elbow hanging out. And he doesn't honk and start to drive away before she's even reached the door. He gets out, and he smiles at me when Jayne introduces us. Then he shakes Sam's hand likes she's a grownup. Then he punches Jayne on the shoulder—lightly!—and asks if she's ready. But not impatient-like. He's asking, because if she isn't ready, he'll wait, like he's her *friend* or something. I wish Tyler were around to see this. Then I'm glad he's not. Jayne introduces her brother as James, but she calls him Jamie. He calls her Jaynie. Jamie and Jaynie—cute. He looks too tough for any girl to call him such a sissy name, but he lets Jayne call him that.

When they're in his car, he waits for her to buckle up before he drives off. He says something to her and she nods, unrolling her window. He doesn't blast the tunes as soon as he's turned on the ignition. I'm staring like they're animals in a zoo. An older brother and younger sister who get along, who *like* each other.

"Knock-knock!" Jayne yells out the window as James's car pulls away, and she waves to both of us.

"Who's there? Who's there?!" Sammie screams at the departing car.

"We are, Sam," I tell her. "We're hanging around our front yard, about to go through to the other side." And Sam doesn't even roll her eyes. She likes my answer well enough to roll up the ramp to the door.

"Yeah? Well, I'm *in between* outside and inside. You don't know which way I'm going to go, do you?"

Does my little sister know I like girls? Does she know I like this girl? *Do* I like this girl? I think about it. And what her hair might look like when it's not in a ponytail.

Sita's going to go haywire when she hears this, I think. Then I think: drat. And then I think: shit on a stick. By the time I shut the front door behind me, I don't care any more who's right and who's not. I need my best friend. For *shite's sake*.

Sammie lets the door slam into my shoulder as she pushes into the foyer. I yank my boots off but don't follow her into the living room. Not just yet. Instead, I pull out my phone to text Sita. Enough's enough. "u r gr8. i am duh. sooo SRRY! i MSS U!"

My thumb pauses in the air above "send." Do I really want to broadcast a full apology to her? On the one hand, there's no point being only half-way contrite. I want Sita back, even if she doesn't seem to miss me. On the other hand, how come *she* can let years and years of friendship just drop away without a second thought? Probably too busy with Daz's tongue down her throat. Not fair, but I now know how distracting a good kissing session can be. Maybe as soon as we get back together, we'll have a world of catching up, and me liking girls will be the least of our worries—like before, when mostly what we talked about was boy-related. I straighten up and press "send"— and the Mom Police snatches my cellphone out of my hand. I've been standing in the hallway, texting. The hallway! Months and months of faultless covert operations, and I blow it in broad daylight!

She's caught me with a cellphone that I'm not authorized to own. She confiscates the phone. She screams a lot. I'm grounded for two weeks, like I'm a kid or something! And I can't even tell Sita about it till the next day.

The next day, we don't have a single class together. Sita avoids the entire lunch room, not just our table, and she's in rehearsal right after school. Even if she calls the house tonight, I won't be allowed to talk to her. Mom hasn't noticed that my friendship life has all but evaporated. She's only interested in punishment and penalty. But when did she ever, specifically, say: "No cellphones allowed!"? She didn't, but I'm smart enough not to point that out. Not yet, anyway. Mom slams a lot of pots around while making supper. After dinner, I clean up by myself while Sammie and Tyler watch sitcoms in the living room.

Thing is, even before Mom found the phone, the parentals acted like they didn't trust me. I'm not allowed to be out late, not allowed to go to mixed parties, I can only go to a friend's house in the evening if they know where it is and whose parents will be around and if Sita's also going (because, what, Sita is a good chaperone? Please!). And if I'm ever late getting home, I don't get to go to that friend's place again. Ever. Which explains why I don't have so many close friends, right? That and having to head home even before Cinderella time, just in case the bus gets a flat or there's a fender-bender causing a traffic jam on the way home.

"When you grow up and have to keep a job, getting in late, even with an excellent excuse, doesn't cut it, missy," my father told me a week ago when I pleaded my case for being given a later curfew. "Missy," like he'd forgotten my name in the heat of his lecture.

And now the Mom Police catches me cell-handed. All my lifelines, disappearing one by miserable one.

IDJIT ALERT: AFTER GETTING HOLD OF A CELLPHONE WITHOUT PARENTS BEING THE WISER, SHE ACTUALLY TEXTS AN APOLOGY TO SITA WHILE STANDING IN THE MIDDLE OF ENEMY TERRITORY, BLITHELY WAVING CELLPHONE IN PLAIN SIGHT!

CHAPTER SEVENTEEN

The next day, a dentist cancels my shift, so I don't even have the distraction of cleaning tooth crap to take my mind off my miserable life. Just home, and more homework.

Except, when I get close to the house, I hear:

"Knock-knock."

"Who's there?

"Anita."

"Anita who?"

"Ah-need-ta stop telling knock-knock jokes!"

We all hang around on the doorstep till the last of the Chinook whispers away. One meeting and I'm smitten. Yeah, terrible word, but that's how I feel: like the sight of her just smited my heart, right on the spot.

So now what? Do I take her hand? Do I whip out a laminated nametag declaring my sexual identity and pin it suggestively on my chest? Ha. I'm unsure how to get something going when I like someone. Do things always start with a kiss? How weird would it be to reach out and hold her hand? What if she's not a lesbian? Or (way worse), what if she is, but just isn't into *me*? I lean in a bit so my shoulder brushes against hers. Jayne's jacket smells a bit like patchouli.

Sammie gives up on us when the knock-knocks dwindle and

rolls in to set the table before Mom gets home (huh, when did that kid ever *volunteer* for housework?). This leaves me carrying the conversation. I can't ask anything too personal. I looked for her in school today, but no sightings. Was I relieved or frustrated? Something in between. My turn to speak.

"Um, so why'd your parents give you such an unusual spelling of your name?" Brilliant opening, Keira.

But she doesn't retreat from my question, just answers, "On my birth certificate it's just spelled 'J-A-N-E,' but I added the 'y' in grade seven, when I became a feminist." Either she catches the confused look on my face, or she's used to explaining this. "You know, like 'women' spelled 'w-y-m-y-n'?"

"Did they change the official spelling?"

She laughs, "No. Way back in the 1970s, feminists and lesbians started spelling it that way so the word wouldn't be an off-shoot of the word 'men.'" She does the lip-squint thing. "I dunno, I heard about that and just wanted to join that fray. You think I'm weird, right?" She blows her hair out of her eyes, cute bottom lip curled around cuter upper lip.

"Weird for being a feminist in grade seven? Or weird for knowing feminist and lesbian spellings?"

"You know, just, *weird*." And she means it. Like she's worried her overpowering difference will be too much for me. This before she hears about my lust for skating. But *is* this too much for me?

Today's only the third time we've ever talked, including the sweater conversation. Until she said the word lesbian, I didn't know that she was one. And I still don't, not for sure, especially since I haven't seen her hang with any of the "out" gay kids at school. I really don't know if she likes me or not. But I do, suddenly, know that *I* like *her*—I like the lip-squints, how she really looks at Sam when they're joking around, the thoughtful way she tries to answer all my dull questions, and even her glossy ponytail.

For once, I know something about myself: I like a girl. *This* girl.

The sun's trying, but the Chinook has blown out of our lives again. Our butts are getting iced from sitting on the cement steps, but I don't invite her into the house in case she says no. I don't want us to even move. If I did, even if I kept talking while standing beside her, she'd disappear into her brother's car or into the frozen air. Instead, I chat mindlessly about her junior high name change.

"So, there you were, twelve years old, and you just started spelling your name differently? How did you explain that to your parents? How'd you get away with it?"

"Oh, *that* stuff is dead easy," she answers with a slow sweep of her arm. "At the time, my dad and mum just thought I was going through a phase." And then we both crack up, cuz, really, what the hell is it with parents and *phases?*

"So, you don't mind getting into trouble?" She doesn't look like the kind of radical who goes against her parents' wishes, but who knows with this girl?

"Nah," she shifts her bum a bit on the stair. Is she trying to sit closer to me, or is she just arctic cold? "Easier to just do it than to worry."

Now I have to wonder if she's talking about the name-change or the other, bigger, topic? Back when I first started grade seven, I remember staring at girls' boobs, and then getting worried that someone would catch me staring at girls' boobs. But mostly I thought it was cuz I didn't have any. I still don't have much in that area, but these days I know I'm not just staring out of envy.

"It?" I manage, not sure what we're talking about any more.

"Parents. It's way easier to get forgiveness than permission." And I realize she's still in the How-to-Break-the-Rules conversation. Not coming out of any closet that I can see. Jayne gets up and starts to walk to the curb to wait for James. "I made every teacher at school spell my name the new way. They didn't much care, as long as I did my homework. By the time report cards came out, it was already changed in the school office. Maybe my parents thought it was a typo, and then later they couldn't argue that they should have changed it back earlier. Or maybe they liked it. You know, adds character."

Then she tells me that once her mom died, her dad kinda let Jayne be Jayne. My dad's pretty slack with me, compared to my mom, but mostly he likes his daughters to be his girls. I think if I changed my name, he'd be eternally miffed.

James shows up, and this time he doesn't get out, but he turns off the car while he waits. In my family, there's one car, and it's mainly for Dad, so he can drive home in the wee hours and not have to cab it or wait for a bus for eighty-five minutes in the middle of the night. Mom takes the bus to and from work, and even Tyler only borrows the car when he's got an official date. I walk to school and skating and take the bus to the dentist offices. Hm, if Jayne and I ever get to the official dating stage, will James be our chauffeur? That thought makes me snort, which is the last thing Jayne hears as they drive away.

Alone on the curb, I realize that the Mom Police might already be home, wondering why I'm not helping Sam set the table. Or (way worse), she might walk up right now, and catch me... what? Catch me thinking about holding hands with a girl?

Yes, I want to hold Jayne's hand, and I want to get to know her better. Just me and Jayne, huddled together while the rest of the world, so jealous, passes us by.

HET-GIRL ALERT: THINKS JUST HAVING A CRUSH ON A GIRL WHO MIGHT BE A LESBIAN MEANS THE OTHER GIRL SHOULD AUTOMATICALLY LIKE HER BACK.

LESBO ALERT: DOESN'T SEEM TO CARE WHAT THE REST OF THE WORLD THINKS, JUST WANTS TO HOLD THIS GIRL'S HAND, NOW.

CHAPTER EIGHTEEN

Jayne and I share a free get-out-of-Backstrom period on Friday morning. We discover this on Thursday when we run into each other walking up to—and then away from—the lunch room. Sita's in drama rehearsal, Amanda's absent, and I just cannot stomach eating with The Three. So Jayne and I hang around the health-food vending machines (I inhale two energy bars), chatting about what we're taking this semester, which teachers we like, blah, blah, blah. Then she asks about my schedule. Does she mean *after* school? How to explain my after-school job and ice-skating?

As she speaks, she pulls her time-table out of her pocket and shows me her spares. I tell her mine.

"Tomorrow we've got a match," she says, squinting her lips. "Meet you at the Auxiliary Gym doors?"

"You got yourself a date, girl!" I say and wince at the word "date" as I stumble over it, but with no way to stop the sound or take it back once it's left my mouth.

Jayne just grins. "Second period—see ya then."

Next morning, we deke out and spend fifty-two minutes telling each other about our lives. I talk about my too-young-but-not-fun parents and turd of an older brother; she already knows my fabulous younger sister. I tell her about my dental-office cleaning jobs (but leave the summer camp stories for another time), and of course, all about my skating. She tells me her mom died two summers ago. James took a year off school to get a job and help their dad out at home. No way can I picture Tyler putting his get-out-of-home plans on hold to cook and care for Sam and me. Not in a gazillion years. Just the thought makes me dizzy and I collapse against the gym doors, pushing them open to reveal a violent floor hockey game. Jayne and I grab the handle and pull the door closed again, laughing.

"My mom stayed real calm until the end," she says, and we step away from the gym doors. "She was the religious one, but my dad got much more devout after Mom left us." Since the funeral, they've been going to church three times a week. "We're a no-smoking, no-drinking, no-swearing, no-dancing family," she tells me. In their church, girls aren't allowed to wear makeup, and they're not really supposed to wear jeans, either. In fact, Jayne's dad thinks not wearing a dress to school is Jayne's way of acting out. Letting her "act out" by wearing jeans is how he shows he's a lenient parent. Wowsa, I may have to give Mom some slack.

And even though James is Jayne's best friend, she can't tell him about her true self. "Not yet, anyway," she informs me, like it's all part of her coming-out plan. Yes, Jayne is into girls. She tells me: "I'm a queero-lesbo," and doesn't flinch or squint or run allllllll the way home.

Now I'm supposed to say, "Me too," and then we'll kiss. "Do you have a plan for *exactly* when you're going to tell your dad and James ... that?" I ask her instead, too shy or cowardly or whatever to even name what "that" is. The hallway is mostly abandoned at this hour, but chocolate bar wrappers and dusty class notes litter the floor. She points at a large room next to the gym doors, crammed full with sports equipment.

"Well, I don't know that it'll be on a Friday at 3:45 three years from today or anything like that, but I do have a plan." We hide behind the football gear piled up for practice. Okay, not hiding exactly, but nobody besides football players wants to be around smelly jerseys and mud-caked shin pads. "You wanna hear my plan?" And she squishes her lips to the left, like this is serious business.

"I want to hear all your plans," I tell her. And it's true. Turns out, I don't just miss having someone to talk to, I miss the listening part too.

"Okay. The big picture. Here goes." And she squishes her lips to the right this time and gives me her strategy: First, finish high school (obviously), then take a year off to work full time. Tell her dad and brother that she's saving to attend their church college. "If I totally scrimp and am really frugal, at the end of that year I'll have enough money saved to move out on my own. And that's when I'll tell them. They'll hate me for a while. My dad says being gay is the worst sin of all sins."

"But James is different, isn't he?" I ask. "He supports you, right?"

"Not about this. James loves me. He *really* loves me. But finding out about the real me will push him over the edge. Big time. But eventually, he'll forgive me, don't you think?" she asks. A football topples from above us, and slams into the floor, bouncing at our heads in a zigzag, stopping at her left knee.

"Of *course* he'll forgive you," I reassure her and use this as an opportunity to put my hand on her shoulder. And I believe my own words because James really does love his Jayne; I've seen it.

"And I'll be eighteen, so they'll maybe even think of me as a legal adult, right?" She says this part with a laugh, cuz families never seem to see us as anything but perpetual kids.

"You'll be almost nineteen?" Yes, I'm fishing for her birthday. Mine is mid-January, so I'm older than most of my classmates. Backwards though I am in the hooking-up department, I'll be the first in my class to hit legal maturity.

"Well, my birthday's in May, but I accelerated grade three, so I'll only be seventeen when I finish high school. Just barely."

Crap on a cracker. Okay, I know this is petty, but this detail throws me for a loop. I was kind of hoping that my first-ever encounter with a girl would be with an *older* girl (hence the Dianne crush), so I'd have someone experienced leading the way. If I'm the older girl, am *I* supposed to lead the way?

When the bell rings, I think: "Saved. By. The. Bell," and I'm happy to rush back to Social Studies. Okay, not *happy*, exactly, but not entirely dreading the pop quiz Mr Rempel has planned as Jayne and I get up, shove the football on top of some stacked goal posts, and head off to our different classrooms.

This whole week has been a series of take-home exams, mid-term essays, and "surprise-it's-not-a-surprise" quizzes. Since losing Sita, my time has been full of blanks anyway, and I racked up a few A-minus grades to balance out the lower grades that will slip in while I'm concentrating on Regionals. Assuming the Mom Police still lets me compete. So far, I'm allowed out for practice. All I've done is study, hit the skating rink even *earlier*, go to my part-time jobs, and go to bed the same time Sam does. A pukey fortnight. But now I have Jayne's company to look forward to. And a potential future kiss. On the lips. With a girl.

Huh. The prospect of getting a girlfriend still seems more scary than joyful. Maybe I should have grabbed Jayne's hand as we ran through the stairwell together? But like I said, the bell saved me from having to decide who was going to be the coach and who the trainee. Sheesh. At least today I'll get to talk to my best friend, again. By now, she'll have gorged on my apology text like it's a plate of cookies.

So I give Sita a little wave when I walk into Social Studies, and then a much bigger one, and finally an arm-beckon. She doesn't even blink, just flips open her textbook and thwacks her pencil against its pages. Obviously, she hasn't accepted my apology. After Rumpled collects our exam booklets, Max points at Sita and makes a joke about her being the perfect choice to play a second-rate singer. Not that funny, but half the class laughs. Including me.

"Max, don't you wish," Sita says quietly, "that you'll someday get popular enough to stop trying to make everyone think you're popular?"

Today is the two-week anniversary of our not-friendship. And I not only texted Sita first, but I tossed out a total remorse message (and not a wimpy "I'm sorry your feelings are hurt," either, but a true, "I take the blame" type of apology). And that was *days ago*. She hasn't called my house or waved to me in the halls, and she's still being rude. She's still acting like ...

It suddenly hits me. Sita doesn't know my phone's been confiscated—what if she *did* text me back and is hurt because *I'm* the one not responding? When the bell rings, I drag myself and all my anger to Sita's locker. I need to get this friendship back on track. I see her before she sees me, so I can read that she's not having the best day of her life. When she notices me by her locker, she blinks. That's something, I guess.

"Look, Sita," I start. "I know you think I didn't answer your text, but—" She clutches her books tightly against her chest. Like I'm suddenly a predator, for Pete's sake?

"Which text?" she answers like she can't wait to get out of this conversation.

"You probably sent me a text in the last couple of days," I persist, my chest brimming with hope bubbles. "And I never got it, cuz Mom—"

"I never sent you a text." She sort of nudges my elbow so she can get into her locker. "Why would I send you a text?" And she flips her locker door open, blocking my face. I'm staring at dull metal and she's heaving her books in as if this is the normal way to have a conversation. Maybe this is the only way she'll have a conversation with me. I take a step back.

"Yeah, why would you?" I ask the locker door. And by the time she slams it shut, I've already gone down the hall and out the door to another blank Friday. Grounded for one more weekend. No texting with Sita, no phoning Jayne, no hanging out with anyone my age. Good thing my parents screwed up on the birth control, cuz without Sam in my life I'd really go crazy right now.

Trudging home, I wonder if maybe Mom snatched away the phone *just as* I was pressing "send." Maybe Sita never got my apology and thinks I'm still mad. Except I *know* I hit "send." I saw the bars light up, which means Sita's so done with me that even a full apology won't bring her back. All through these past two weeks, I truly believed that Sita and I have (had) a better friendship than this fight. Stronger. That one of us would come round and bring the other one with her. But now even that hope bubble has popped.

At home, Sammie and I play Fiddler's Faddle till it's time to set the table. I do the plates and Sammie whizzes around placing the forks and knives right beside each other. At dinner, Tyler natters away about his great football practice, about how great *he* was in football practice. Nobody notices that I'm sad. Nobody cares. Until Sam pipes up: "Can we invite Keira's girlfriend over for supper on Sunday?"

Six eyes swivel toward me. Tyler looks like he's going to sneeze, which means he's thinking hard. Probably digging deep so he can revive his childhood "lezzie" insults. The Mom Police just looks like this is the next thing she's been waiting for, her eyes wide and crinkled at the same time. Like grounding is a hassle-free holiday compared to what I'm getting next.

"Keira's grounded till midnight on Sunday, so no friends for supper," Dad pipes in. Then he genuinely saves me from whatever mean words Mom is about to spout. "And Samantha, some girls call their friends 'girlfriends,' but you should save that word for the dates Tyler goes on after he plays winning games." And then Dad winks at me, like Sammie's too young to understand grownup language. I've never been so happy for a parent to be so wrong.

IDJIT ALERT: DO I REALLY NEED TO SPELL IT ALL OUT, HERE?

CHAPTER NINETEEN

"You have to make up with Sita," Jayne announces, once I've told her the short and pathetic story of sorta coming out to my best friend. I tell her just about the part where Sita informs me I like girls and then freaks that I might like her. Or expect her to be like me.

"Are you out of your mind?" I ask. "I don't even know exactly what freaked her out, only that I admitted liking girls. And now we're not friends." As I say the words, I feel our friendship circling down, down, down a drain, and my eyelids feel droopy. "We're done." I add. The Surge story can wait for some other confession box.

Jayne's walking home with me. Long before Mom (or even Sam) gets home, she'll call James to pick her up. Again. And he won't mind. Again. We can spot Sammie's bus coming from where we sit, but I'm still nervously crumbling yellow leaves in my hands, waving the red ones like miniature flags.

Last night I heard Mom and Dad talking about my recent troubles. That's the phrase they used, "Keira's recent troubles." Like they actually noticed something about my life? Like I'm a big worry to them? Gimme a break!

If I sit right beside the heating vent in the bathroom, I can hear their voices climb the pipes from their bedroom. They sleep in the basement—they took over the rumpus room shortly after Sam was born—so kids and parents can each have our own floor. This is a sweet arrangement, as they don't talk about anything important until after bedtime. On nights when Dad's not working late, that is.

I don't always listen; mostly, they talk about what shifts Dad has coming up, if Mom's doing overtime. Boring grownup gab. But last year, after Mom had been especially tough on all of us at dinner, I crawled into the bathroom and huddled over the vent, just in case. I heard Dad say, "Samantha." And Mom said, "Three hundred bucks a lineal metre." They were talking about the ramp we needed up to our front steps for Sammie's new motorized wheelchair. A new ramp, big deal. We all use it, even the guy who delivers mail every day. So, yeah, most of their post-bed conversations are dull, but tonight I had to hear what they'd say.

Because I'm used to waking up so early, I almost fall asleep with my ear resting on the bathroom floor waiting for them to climb into bed. My neck cricks, and my ear gets chilly, but it's worth it. Mom's voice creeps into my ear and rouses me, bad-mouthing me, natch.

"Look, I know Samantha's young," Mom starts in, "but maybe she's picking up on something about Keira that we're not."

A grunt from Dad. He doesn't want to have this conversation any more than I do.

"Why would Samantha call this new girl Keira's girlfriend, unless Keira said something?" Mom is nothing if not persistent. Does she really think I'd be idjit enough to use the word "girlfriend" out loud? In this house, with Tyler always in ear range? As if.

"It's just a word, darl, don't get your panties in a bunch." Dad always knows when a joke will side-track Mom's zeal.

It works, sorta: Mom laughs, but her voice sounds tight, like she's forcing herself into pleasant mode. "Okay," she concedes, "but

I still think we should have a talk with her."

The sound of floorboards and bedcovers. I don't know how Dad does it, but on nights when he doesn't work, he still crawls into bed to match my mother's schedule. But right now, he'd rather be sleeping than having *this* conversation. I can tell because he snaps the blankets hard and clicks the light off.

Mom continues. "Keira's nearly sixteen. Don't forget she's older than most of her classmates, and—"

"Absolutely not." Dad cuts her off before she can finish. He switches the light on again. Uh-oh, Dad's got a mean streak that comes out when he's tired. If Mom keeps it up, we'll all be tip-toeing around tomorrow morning. "Being older than her friends doesn't mean she's more confused, quite the opposite. She's had time to grow up, and she's just taking her time in the dating game." Then I hear the rustling newspaper, which means Dad will catch up on the day's news while Mom drifts off.

"Dating?" Mom sounds shocked that this is even a possibility. Come on, at my age, she'd already gone out (that's what teenagers called it in the olden days) with two different boys. And hadn't even met Dad yet.

"It's a good thing she's got a new friend. She was spending too much time with Sita." It strikes me that Dad's a lot like James: he loves me, but he doesn't entirely want to know me. I shift my bum around. Mom mumbles something I don't quite catch.

"Keira shouldn't get too close to any girl, period," Dad says. "High school's all about meeting new people, expanding your friend horizon." "Friend horizon"—who speaks like that?

"Fine, you win," Mom says through a yawn (she's been saying that a lot, lately), and I hear her snap off the light again.

Then I get out fast, before I hear any post-lights-out noises. Ew-www.

Back in my room, I huddle in bed, thoughts of Surge and Sita and Jayne and Mom's spidey senses going around and around inside my skull. Sammie sleeps securely through my alarm, little baby snores escaping her throat.

I'm glad Dad trusts me. Yeah, okay, his trust is based on a giant, inflated lie, but I'll deal with that later. They think Sita and I are not hanging out together just cuz we're in high school now? Huh, how does that work? Makes me wonder if Mom had friends she ditched when they were teens because she was getting too old, too fast. No way I'm bringing Jayne around here for family supper. Not ever.

And I actually fall asleep thinking about what it would be like to undo Jayne's ponytail and rub my face into her loose, perfectly straight hair.

Two days later, Jayne walks me home again. We sit where we can spy Mom coming home or Sam's bus dropping her off, perched on the hill that slopes up to the Razma's house. Mr and Mrs and another Mr Razma—I could never figure out if he was a brother or border or poor relation. Or some other kind of other.

For extra cash, I shovel their walk in winter and rake their leaves in fall. Maybe that's why they've never chased me and Sita away when we plant our bums for hours on the small ledge in their grass, a perfect post-school gossip hillock. Bringing Jayne here feels like I'm cheating on Sita, which reminds me about what my dad said last night. Maybe he's right. Maybe Jayne just needs a new high school friend? I have no evidence that she wants to kiss me. And I'm pretty sure I've iced-over how much I want to kiss her. Could Dad be right that Sita and I are only mad at each other because we were too close? But how close is too close?

Jayne knocks on the stiff grass, and I say "Who's there?" automatically. We both crack up and lie back laughing so hard a button pops off my shirt, which makes us laugh even harder. Jayne reaches over and puts her hand on my forearm. We're not holding hands, but she didn't shove my shoulder buddy-like, either. That graze of her fingers makes the Chinook return, and it whooshes into my belly.

"Did you know that Leonardo da Vinci could write with one hand and draw with the other?" she asks. "I can sit in class and trace a mermaid and still bark atlas facts at Rumpled."

"Um..." Is she waiting for me to counter? "Did you know that Alan Shepard the astronaut smuggled a golf ball and club onto the spacecraft so he could play golf on the moon?" The only non-skating sport fact I know.

Jayne's face isn't pretty the way Talia Sitkins is pretty, but Jayne's face invites my whole attention. I'm frozen and on fire at the same time, my insides made up of murky ice and furious flames. Is *this* how bi feels? Truth be true, almost every kid I know is all a-okay with gay people—as long as it's no one we know. Gay people are fine out there in the grownup world (Max Bledsoe has mentioned his "art-fag" cousin who studies film at UBC at least twelve times). And gay people are safely hilarious when they're contained inside television. But my school has about 700 kids, and only seven are out, when the stats say it should be more like seventy. Gay is great, and queer is quasi-cool. Just surf the web or tune in to every single sit-com for the latest version of the gay best-friend character. S'long as you're living on the other side of the city. If you're sitting next to someone from my school in the lunch room, then you damn well better be straight as a geometry ruler.

There are probably a lot of kids like Jayne (like me) who may be gay, but you can't tell just from looking at them. Boys who dress up too nicely may get picked on, but nobody thinks the teasing is for real. And girls who don't wear makeup or *enough* makeup, or who wear plain T-shirts and blue jeans, may get called "dyke," but no one really notices them enough to care.

Yes, I'm a superficial jerk. I should have noticed Jayne long before she appeared in my front yard: that lip-twist thing she does is adorable, she moves her arms in a flowing way that makes me long for her to wrap them around me, and her eyes look like avocadoes when she talks about anything important to her, which includes her brother, how she spells her name, her plans for three years from now (yikes, I can't even think past Regionals!), and even how to get away with wearing jeans all the time when her father thinks a good, church-going girl should wear dresses.

Jayne shows me her blue jean artwork. Her hands trace across her jeans like tapered wands, each fingertip dripping with myths and magic and burgundy-coloured ink. (Yes, I am smitten.) The thing about Jayne is that her jeans, like her name, are all personalized. On this pair, she's drawn water nymphs all over the pockets, with waves spilling over the folds. On another, she tells me, she's drawn the story of Iphis—who was born a girl but lived as a boy—inked from front to back to front, all along where the belt would loop around. Partly because the ink wouldn't show up and partly because her brother says they look slutty, she doesn't ever wear black jeans. But blue jeans are just homey enough for her to get away with. Jayne says she wears her shirt untucked when she leaves her house, but tucked in by the time she gets to school. Jayne is an amazing artist.

With my pinky finger, I follow a water nymph's hair as it wraps itself around and around her thigh. The etchings make her jeans look like the ice does after the first round of a competition. "But how *do* you get away with being, you know, *you*, without your dad taking over your life?"

"Dishonesty," she answers, pulling out a pen and beginning to draw a hydra along the inside seam of her jeans. "My dad and my brother love me, but they don't really see me, not the details." She draws miniature scales onto the skin of the tiny reptile snaking down toward her knees.

"Lying, huh? I shoulda thought of that." And I mean it. Instead of hiding from the world, why not just lie to it? Except, isn't that kinda what I've been doing the whole time?

"Yeah, I don't tell my dad or Jamie who I really am. Not yet." She stops drawing and pulls her legs under her bum. "So my brother makes jokes about how he'll beat up my future husband if he isn't good enough for me." At this Jayne giggles, but it doesn't sound like a very happy giggle. "I shouldn't laugh, James is a great brother." She slides down the hill a bit, so our bums are at the same level. "He's a true believer, you know?"

I nod, though I don't really know. I'm not even sure what church they go to. My parents have never been religious, though I think my dad's parents are Catholic. Tyler and Sam and I haven't ever gone to a church, except as tourists, once.

"In my church, homosexuality is a sin," she explains, like I'm some sort of idjit.

"Yeah, a lot of people think that," I say, nodding some more. "My parents don't go to church, but I'm pretty sure my dad thinks being a lesbian would be the ultimate felony." I'm getting goose bumps on my belly cuz we're sitting so close together, two normal girls, yakking away about being queer. I've thought about coming out to my parents, and I tried to come out to Sita, but with Jayne we just are who we are.

"If James thought his sister was a lesbian, it would totally wreck him, you know? *Destroy* him. Like I'd betrayed our love."

If Tyler found out that I really was interested in girls, he wouldn't just tease me about being a lesbo, he would out-and-out torture me. But not out of fear. Just another sibling defect for him to strike at.

"Jamie and I are really close. Especially since our mom died." She stops for a minute, and watches a cat creep daintily across the wall between yards. "It's gonna be bad when I tell him." Jayne nods, but like what she's saying is not okay at all. "By then, it'll be too late. I'll be too far gone for him to be able to do anything to save me."

As she shakes her head, I remember how I fell asleep thinking about emancipating her ponytail. That will have to wait.

"So, I'll have to wait," she says, as if she's right there in my head.

"To tell him," she explains. "I'll have to wait till it feels like it's too late."

And—coward that I am—I decide to wait, too. We can have the "Keira's not quite gay and not quite straight" conversation another time. Right now, her worry for her family sends me into a jittery mood. I close my eyes and just breathe for a bit. I smell Jayne's apple oatmeal shampoo, and I hear her pen scratching against her jeans. We lie there for a while, just breathing.

When I open my eyes, the cat's gone, and Jayne has smoothed her sad smile out. I lean back and slide my bum forward, so my head rests on the slight ledge. I'm thinking this would be an excellent chance for Jayne to kiss me. On the one hand, it would be a bold, crazy move. Not only could anyone in the Razma house spot us, but this corner has loads of traffic, and at the bottom of the hill is a stop sign where cars and kids and people walking dogs pause and look up the hill while they're waiting to cross. On the other hand, Jayne's lips ... on my lips. I almost pucker as I think this. And, look, I know, since I'm the one thinking make-out thoughts, I should maybe be the one leaning over and making the moves on *her?*

So I just close my eyes again, shove my hands under my back to make my chest rise a bit higher (what, you think only het-boys like boobs?), and think lusty thoughts. We've got about twenty minutes before Sam's bus grunts up the hill. I am going to fret for the next nineteen minutes if we don't try something, here. I really, really want to melt those minutes away with some kissing.

"Are you just hanging out with me because you miss your best friend?"

"Huh?" I prop myself on my elbows.

"Because it's one thing if you think we're, like, maybe becoming girlfriends, but another if you just miss Sita, and so you need a replacement friend." Ah, now I get why she's urging me to make up with Sita. I could pretend not to understand, but actually what she's saying makes a lot of sense.

"I like you because ... I like you?"

"Hmm. You like me or you like my mouth?"

Spooky—how'd she know? I should have a snappy reply, but I *do* like her mouth, so I brilliantly just beam and keep on sitting next to her.

"Maybe we both need mouth-to-mouth resuscitation," I blurt out. "But for our lying tongues, not for our bitter hearts."

And then we crack up all over again, playfully pushing each other around the hill, eventually rolling all the way down to the curb, just like elementary school mud rats who can't help ourselves.

Maybe Jayne and I are both waiting for the other to make a first move.

HET-GIRL ALERT: THINKS IF TWO LESBIANS START DATING, ONE OF THEM HAS TO BE THE GIRL AND ONE HAS TO BE, WELL, THE LESBIAN.

LESBO ALERT: LONGS TO BE PART OF THIS NEW GIRL-LESBIAN COUPLE SO MUCH MORE THAN SHE WANTS BACK INTO THAT SUMMER BOY-GIRL COUPLE.

BISEXUAL ALERT: STILL, SORTA, KINDA WANTS TO BE PART OF A BOY-GIRL COUPLE. EVENTUALLY. MAYBE.

CHAPTER TWENTY

My BIG NEWS: I kissed a girl.

I kissed a girl, and that kiss still floats on my lips. That kiss lifts my feet when I execute a perfect Axel this morning and feeds me when I skip lunch to run over to Sammie's school and deliver her forgotten "Make Like a Leaf" autumn project. That kiss reminds me that my body isn't my enemy but can be my friend, and not just when I'm skating. That kiss makes me love my new school, my parents, my skating competitors. And that kiss reminds me that Sita's my best friend, that with best friends, it doesn't matter who said what or whether or not my apology was good, *we're* good. Or we're going to be good. After school, I'll go to the drama room and make her make friends with me. That Jayne kiss fixes everything.

There's no one in my life to tell this to. I actually thought about texting Surge, but even I am not that much of an idjit to text, eye kist uh gyrl!!!!!!!

Actually, the girl kissed me. Yes, Jayne made the first move. We rolled down the Razmas' hill and landed in a jumble of arms and legs, and I think my wrist grazed against her boob. But we'd rolled crookedly, so we were jammed up against the hedge that borders the alley. No pedestrians, not even the cat. Every part of me wanted to stay inside that jumble, but I knew we'd have to separate soon. I started to say, "You grabbing my ass?" because I wanted to sound witty and casual, not desperate, and definitely not *virginal*.

Except Jayne stroked my left cheek, her finger etching onto my face the story of Iphis falling in love and transforming into a boy so that she could marry Ianthe. She grazed her knuckles along my lips, and I felt them quiver. When Surge kissed me, I wasn't expecting it, and I got lost in the first full-on kiss I'd ever had in my life. I didn't know he liked me (cuz maybe it was an "end of summer, may as well kiss someone" kiss), and I didn't even know if I liked him (cuz maybe it was a "how can I know if I like girls or boys if I haven't kissed either?" kiss), but then we were deep inside each other's mouths. And didn't climb out until we boarded separate buses the next day. Or that's how my lips seem to remember those last twelve hours of summer.

Jayne's lips don't taste like candy or a fruit bowl or the back of my hand. Jayne's lips taste like the rollercoaster at the Stampede and a thick comforter in winter. They taste like I'll keel over onto my back if I don't get another.

Jayne's lips ... still kissing mine as I say, "Wait, someone might see, better stop." And I pull away too fast.

She shakes out of our jumble and has her cellphone out before I can push my words back down my traitor throat.

The problem with fixes: they can be rebroken.

In the hallway just before Social Studies, Sita walks right past me and over to Talia Sitkins's locker, hugs her, and skips off with her new best mate. I get that she's making friends with other girls who aren't me, but—Talia Sitkins? My brain does a toe-flip and falls—splat—bottom-first on the ice-hard linoleum. And, forget yesterday's kiss, all my resolve collapses into itself, just because Sita's talking with some other girl. Queer, eh?

Back in September, Sita and I planned to take Sammie Trick-or-Treating around the neighbourhood this Hallowe'en, right before heading over to the dance at the school. Take Sam trick-or-treating, Sita at the Regionals to cheer me on, and me there for the opening of her play. In each scenario, Sita's there for me to talk to.

Except now, she isn't here to talk to. For the first time. Ever.

Before all this happened, back in early summer, I took the plunge and asked Sita point-blank about kissing. Just in case she was right about me meeting someone while playing junior ranger, I wanted to get some solid kissing advice.

"What if I do meet the cutest person, and that someone actually wants to make out with me?" (Thinking back on that day, I realize I've been hiding my pronouns for a very long time with Sita.) "And what if my breath tastes like last night's supper?"

"You telling me my breath smells bad?"

"Not *you*, *me*." We were filling in magazine surveys. I munched through my third apple in a row, and Sita finished off a total of one grape. Totalling her scores in these quizzes ("Can You Flirt Your Way to Popularity?" or "Match the Celebrity Tattoo to the Celebrity Belly!") is the only math Sita really gets into. Her sisters buy these magazines in bundles and pass them along down the line.

"Um, brush your teeth in between meals?"

"Thanks, but I'm serious!"

"Me, too." Sita puts the mag down, checking off her fingers. "Brush after meals, brush in the morning, pop a piece of gum or chocolate in your mouth right after lunch break or whenever you think you might run into a cute guy." She leaves the mag on the ground, holding out her palms in front of her. "But this whole give-me-advice-on-how-to-avoid-mouth-drool is not your real question, is it?" (I hadn't even thought about mouth-drool—gross.)

Me: "No."

Sita: "Okay, so, the idea of full-on sex grosses you out? So don't have sex. Even with a guy you're totally into."

Me: "But it's not that simple. What am I supposed to do, go kiss anyone I have a crush on, take their lips for a test-drive, then hop off until I figure out who I really like?"

Sita: "In a nutshell? Yes. Take lips on test drives. If you don't like kissing them, trust me, you won't like anything else they do with their bodies."

Me: "But—"

Sita: "Yeah." The end of that conversation. And Sita and I haven't had another one like it since. May never again.

Maybe thinking about Sita giving me kissing advice makes me maudlin (or maybe just thinking about needing kissing advice during my kiss with Jayne makes me maudlin). Or maybe ...

❋

After Sita chooses Talia over me, I head home. Get there just as Tyler and his buds head out to shoot hoops.

"Hey, it's Stickbean!" Genius Jason says to me as they're heading out the door.

Tyler's always practicing his sports—with the guys, by himself, with Sammie. Since skating is my only sport, the only other exercise I get is in gym class. In Backstrom High, gym is only mandatory for grade ten. Which is a relief to everyone. Kids who are good at sports, like Tyler, try out for teams. And kids who hate athletics no longer have to suffer through Dodgeball and Pom-Pom-Tag and Steal-the-Bacon.

But I don't mind gym. Because of skating, I don't have the time (or, let's face it, the talent) for any other organized sports. And in gym, we run around throwing things at each other and get to take a shower in the middle of the day. It beats another class on the history of the class system in Western Europe.

Everyone's least favourite team sport is field hockey. In my class, the girls whine about having to play outside, especially when it gets too cold (too cold, ha! try skating before dawn on a February morning when it's already minus 35 degrees Celsius!). And it bugs my classmates that the sticks have a "right" side and a "wrong" side.

"What kind of hockey is this?" Talia yells out to Ms Mukerjee. "In real hockey, in *Canadian* hockey, players are allowed to hit the puck with either side of the stick."

Yeah, like Talia has ever played ice hockey in her life. All her expertise comes from watching her current boyfriend's hockey games. His team is so good, they get the prime arena practice time: every afternoon from four till six, Saturday afternoons from noon till four. He scores; she cheers. So apparently she's an expert.

The "Canadian" emphasis is because Ms Mukerjee has an accent. A *British* accent. But Talia thinks that anyone not from around here must somehow get the rules of hockey wrong, no matter that field hockey is *not* originally Canadian. If Sita were out there with us, Talia would get a blast of sarcasm to match her unwitty complaints. But Sita and I don't share gym class. Looks like we don't share anything any more.

LESBO ALERT: LIKES FIELD HOCKEY.

HET-GIRL ALERT: THINKS FOCUSSING ON SCHOOL SPORTS WILL DISTRACT HERSELF FROM THE **KISSING A GIRL** THING.

CHAPTER TWENTY-ONE

Famed Hollywood dancer Ginger Rogers (yes, the '30s also crack me up), once said that women have to do whatever men do, only backward and in high heels. She was talking about dancing, but she was *really* talking about everything. And she's dead-right. Except in skating.

The real reason I don't enter pairs competitions is because your partner has to lift you over his shoulders. Even at the Regionals, you have to be wicked strong to lift another person while you're gliding around on knife-thin blades. Women have way harder moves, and we have to be flashier, but guys have to jump and spin *and* carry weight. I may not have many curves, but there aren't any boys strong enough to lift my five-foot, eight-inch frame. And there certainly aren't any girls who can throw me over their heads and then catch me on my way down. It's hard enough getting my skate-heavy foot above my own head for the Biellman spin, where I hold the blade in both hands and arch my back. Maybe that's why too many people think male ice skaters are gay: the guys have to sweat like grunts, but at the same time dance around the ice like they're dainty.

Twice this fall, I have taken a serious ... fall. The third time, Winnie happens to be observing to give me notes, standing in toasty-warm boots with a note pad. I spin counter-clockwise so hard, I spin onto my left ass-cheek. Hard. I hear clapping coming from somewhere in the bleachers. Hockey players waiting their turn for the ice. "Ignore them," Winnie tells me, "focus on the problem you're having."

The problem is, I'm letting these falls get to me. Or I'm letting everything else get to me, and the pressure is making me fall.

"You don't know about pressure," Winnie says, dismissing the dramatics of my swan-dive.

"I'm not trying to make excuses, just saying that's why my timing is off," I tell her, wiping ice shavings off my cheek and lips. The shavings taste like exploded bits of Pop Rocks. "I'm going to a new school, and I've got new worries. Different worries," I tell her. I'm about to describe those worries in detail.

"Ha," is Winnie's sympathetic reply. "Life is pressure." I swear she does the Sita hand wave. Missing your best friend means missing even her most irritating habits.

I try to concentrate on what Winnie's telling me. After all, the Regionals are this coming weekend. I need to come in at least third place to advance to the Provincials in January, a week after my sixteenth birthday. Before boys, before girls, before Sita even, skating was my first love. I have to focus on *that* romance. Right now.

Back to my routine. Winnie let me go with Avril Lavigne's "Complicated," even though it's from eons ago. But the song switches from fast to glide-y to fast again, and the lyrics suit me. Winnie shifted some of my jumps around to give me more of a breather between my flashiest moves, but mostly she leaves composing the routine to me. She knows I can get any jump or spin down to perfection, as long as I rehearse it enough. As long as I let myself live inside the routine instead of just following the routine.

The way I practice is to repeat each complicated move till I can do them all in order: no music, no decorations, simply jump, jump, leap, spin, leap. Then I add the waltzing, the three-turns, the linking moves that let me sweep across the rink and look pretty while doing so. When I've added in every minor flourish, I get through the entire routine slowly. Then I skate it over and over and over and over. I skate till I'm not following a program, I'm the very essence of skating itself. Till I don't have to think any more, I just *do*. Till the routine is skating me.

Some skaters flinch or choke during competitions. Too much pressure to execute every single jump perfectly, to maintain a centred spin, to not bobble any toe loops. That pressure ripples the icy air and caves their spirit. Some skaters listen to the do-or-die tune, some fail one Axel and skim through the rest of their routine listlessly. Winnie believes I'm an intergalactic meteor because my competitive routines shine so brilliantly. As long as my feet scrape across this frosted mirror and scissor through air, as long as I can stroke the ice, I'm the Calgary Stampede parade in February, a snowstorm in July, and the Winter Olympics every day.

After Winnie gives me some more practical tips—"Not pressure, but release; not your body in two directions, but in every direction at once"—I skate through the routine again, not thinking, not even feeling, just letting the ice seep into my blood. My blades swish and my arms wave at the top row of bleachers. My hair lashes the boards, my hips spin and circle and twist. One toe shatters down and one leaps straight up. A winter carnival of a jump. A tsunami between destruction and creation. Magic.

When I leave the ice on Friday morning, I think I'm ready. I *know* I'm ready. And not just for the competition tomorrow. I'm ready for Jayne's poised lips.

❈

After that "my lips just did a triple-loop and when can we do it again?" first kiss, Jayne and I don't kiss again for days. Almost a full week! My lips drift through winter to spring and back to winter again, as I wait for her lips to etch out the seasons in ink or cirrus clouds or Saskatoon berries. Waiting for the softest of snowfalls to scrawl stories onto my skin. Onto the skin of my skin.

When we pass in the hallways, she chews her lips and I wave, then duck into my physics class, or I nod and she shakes her ponytail. Every day, we're communicating in code. At lunch, she eats with her friends, and I settle down with The Three.

So on Hallowe'en, I decide that maybe I'm waiting for her and she's waiting for me. "Walk me home?" I ask when she's at the drinking fountain, and she skips the bus ride that Friday. How could I have ever called her Plain Jane? When Jayne squishes her lips to one side, whatever's inside my chest bounces zigzag against my ribs. For most of the walk, we chat about her brother (applied to and got accepted into a draughting program) and Sita. While we walk, the backs of my knuckles slip against the back of her knuckles.

"She's freaked out about my liking girls. But also …" I flinch at the part that's so hard. "Sita wants me to like boys, but if I can't be that, then I should be totally lesbian. For totally sure."

"You're saying you're not out? Are you're saying you haven't even entered a closet to come out of?"

"Huh?" My suave comeback.

"You into girls or not?"

No layback spin will get me out of this conversation. Hmm. Maybe I should add a second layback to my routine? Judges are always so impressed that figure skaters can perform moves that make astronauts dizzy. I remember to nod at Jayne, but I've taken too many seconds to respond to her question. She's unfolded her arms and started to walk away from me. I follow. Jayne's walking in the direction of my house, so before she gets there, I decide to *show* her how I feel. My body works so much better than my mouth does, right? "Flaunt your strengths," Winnie always says. "Tilt into your best stuff."

I run to catch up and give her hip a nudge when I reach her side. She bites her lips—good sign! So, without really thinking too much about my plan, I grab the belt loop in her jeans and pull her into the alley just behind my house.

"Happy Freak Day!" I whisper into her ear, pull our hips together, and press my breasts into hers. Triple axel bliss. I bend to kiss the side of her earlobe. Only the side of her earlobe, because she moves away as I'm zeroing in. "Hey, I'm not trying to be funny," I say to her, "I want to—"

"Yeah, I know what you're trying," she says, pulling away from the wall and heading back to the sidewalk. She doesn't look mad, but she certainly doesn't look turned on.

We climb the hill to my house. "Are you mad?" Maybe I *am* supposed to wait for her to pick the right moment. She kissed me last time. Maybe she's in charge of kissing from now on? I'm confused and horny and feeling a little embarrassed and a lot rejected. Is this what boys have to go through? Am I going to have to be more sympathetic to Tyler?

"I'm not mad, Keira, I'm just ... You're not ready to kiss me yet. Not really." She sighs like it's so complicated it might take years to explain. "Knock-knock."

"Who's there?

"Kip."

"Kip who?"

"Kip your hands to yourself, girl!"

We're at the ramp at the front of the house. I walk up, unlock the door, and head for the kitchen, not sure if Jayne will follow me. She does.

"Want a snack?" I ask. Partly to be polite, because Mom always says when it's your place, you're the hostess, no matter who comes to visit. And partly to say something, rather than demand what the hell she's talking about, and how does *she* know what I'm ready for?

"No thanks." She sits at the top of the stairs that lead down to my parents' bedroom, maybe waiting for me to either invite her into my bedroom or to kick her out.

I know I'm too scared to join the Gaysta Club (sorry, but that's what the kids at Backstrom call it). I know I'm not brave enough to hold her hand in the school halls or walking down the street near my house or at the mall or the coffee shop—or anywhere, really. No, scratch all that. I want to hold her hand from the moment before I wake up until I flop onto the bed at night. I want to hold her hand when I'm skating alone and when I'm in Mr Grier's lethal literature lessons. I want to skate while holding her hand at the Olympics, and I want to slow-dance with her at the school dance she's not allowed to attend. I *want* to, but ...

S'long as we're alone, hidden behind bushes, no one else elbowing into our couple-fest. Then, what I want to do with Jayne flares into x-rated territory (x-rated for virgin-me, that is). With Surge, the kissing was the starting point. With Jayne, the kissing is the rest of the routine, the beginning and the middle and the grand finale. With Jayne, I want our kissing to be figure-eight infinity. But I'm scared. So I look around in the fridge, searching for the perfect snack to offer my almost-girlfriend, rather than making sentences out of the "bi, bi, bi" struggling to propel out of my mouth.

Jayne wants more from me than a half-baked "I'm not sure, yet." But I'm *not* sure, yet.

Even without Sita around, I've figured out that I aimed my crush at Dianne because there was no way anything would happen. For weeks I could fire lesbionic lust in her direction and not end up kissing her. Truth be true, if I'd had a crush on Surge, I would've probably screwed that up on purpose, too.

But Jayne is not Dianne. Jayne knows ancient mythology and can draw hidden stories and has her entire life planned out so she can get to be who she already knows she is. In the kitchen, I open and close cupboard doors, wash an apple, peel an orange. I stand in the kitchen doorway and see Jayne, only a few feet away, sitting very still. She's waiting for me to stop waiting. She's waiting for me to join her, not just by sitting on the steps, but at her parade into the future.

Jayne likes me, and that alone should send me running out of the kitchen to grab her shoulders and shout out loud. But I can't lie to her.

From the stairwell, she calls out, "No more kissing. Not until you decide who you truthfully are." She means until I've laminated my full-on "out-and-proud" membership card. But that's so unfair, because *she's* not even entirely out yet.

"Look, maybe I wasn't entirely ready for you before, but you kissed me anyway." I've brought grape juice and two plastic cups with me, but my hands shake, so I put the bottle down beside us. I wipe my damp hand on my forehead. The cold feels good. "But I do know I want to kiss you again."

She's holding herself very still, like my words might hurt her. But isn't *she* the one trying to get me to skate around in only one kind of rink?

"Jayne, I *really* want to kiss you again." I sit down right beside her, hip to hip. "It's not that I'm unsure about you, I'm just slow when it comes to romance, okay?" I smile, so she sees I'm being Keira the knuckle-headed, mixed-up, teen-girl wonder.

But she's not smiling back. She's not putting her arms around me and taking advantage of the fact that my house that is *never* empty is now occupied by just the two of us. "Look, Keira," she twirls her hair between two fingers. "I'm not trying to out you, and I don't want to preach about who you tell and when. But you don't want to tell *any-body*. Besides Sita—who told you, and not the other way around— who knows you like girls? You don't even tell your sister, and she loves you to pieces."

"*You* haven't even told your best-friend brother!" I hurl my accusation at her. "Jayne, telling Sita was a big deal, a *huge* deal. We'd never talked about gay things before." I get that Jayne doesn't know who I am, really, but I like her a lot. Why isn't that enough? I'm practically crying, and that, of course, makes me mad. "Why do *I* have to figure out who I'm going to be seventy years from now? If we both like each other, if we *both* have stuff to hide, why can't we just kiss?"

Jayne's shoulders soften a tad. "It's not about waving placards around, I'm not saying that." She turns to meet my gaze. Sitting staring into each other's eyes should be mega-romantic. This is so unfair.

"Maybe *you* are the one too scared to kiss *me*," I cut in. She stiffens, like I've hit something. "This isn't about coming out with a megaphone in the auditorium at a school dance, right?" I'm on a roll. "You wear certain clothes with drawings on them to send signals to people who already know you, but most people remain clueless, right?" Why is my mouth working overtime? Usually, I can't think of any words, but right now the worst ones swoosh out and whip around us. "Teachers don't know who you are, most kids at school don't even know you're a lesbian." Jayne leans farther and farther away from me as I talk, her body practically disappearing into the wall. "And your oh-so-close family members haven't even met you yet; you're saving that truth for when they're as much of your past as I will be!"

Bringing her family into this mess is a low blow. But I want us to get past the part of a relationship that Sita calls the "Pre-make-up break-up." I want to blast us to smithereens, so we can remake ourselves into one smithereen, together. After I've said those fracturing words, I take her hand, to show her that we're in this together.

She lets me take her hand, but she doesn't exactly squeeze back.

"But I *am* out at school, Keira, don't you know that? All the gay kids know, and some others. I just have to keep it from the kids who go to my church." And, even though we're sorta holding hands, the distance between hasn't stopped growing.

"And how exactly do you manage that?" I ask, with as much sarcasm as I can. "It's not like you wear a lesbian nametag or anything. And it's not like you've joined the Gay-Straight Alliance at school."

Backstrom's seven out kids sit together at lunch, and meet up at the coffee shop before classes every morning so they can walk to school together.

"I have, actually," Jayne replies. "Sort of." She looks embarrassed.

"You attend club meetings? You walk with them to the coffee shop before school?" I enquire. "And you've sat at that lunch table?"

"No, but ..." No *way* she's come out at school. Her brother would find out in a fast-forward minute, and Jayne'll go to any length to protect her family from knowing her real self. "Um, I did date one of the members for a couple of months last year." My stomach switches from angry mosquito mode to jealous grasshopper mode. My jealousy is completely unfair, given that I still haven't told Jayne about Surge.

I nudge my leg against hers. Has she had many girlfriends? Why are these questions only occurring to me now? I have a story to tell her about Surge—why should I be surprised that she has stories, too?

Suddenly I lock onto the point of the story: she's had a girlfriend who was out, but didn't out *her*.

I take a deep gulp. "I'll sit at that table," I tell Jayne. Gulp. "I'll sit at that table, and you can come by, and people will only think you're being supportive of that group, like always." Gulp. Once I've joined that table regularly, Tyler will know, every kid in school will know. And Sita won't ever forgive me, *again*. My heart thumps out through my chest and flops onto the stairs.

Jayne's knee relaxes against mine. My heart madly quivers, lying so exposed outside my body, but there's no going back now. "I'll sit there at the Gaysta lunch table. Every lunch period." I'm gonna get creamed. By Tyler and by all the kids at our school who love to harass fresh meat. Dad will thump some furniture around, maybe hit a wall with his fist. Mom will freak out, maybe immerse herself in a baking frenzy and give me lectures about teen sexuality. Endless lectures. And take away from me whatever she thinks is left to take away. Everything except skating, I hope. Sam will just be so happy that she gets to hang out with Jayne some more. And Tyler can't be much worse to me than he is right now, right? He'll just be awful in a different way. Amanda (and maybe even Joline?) will kill me for abandoning our lunch table (and maybe for *why* I abandoned them), but I'll deal with that—

"Ooh, Keira," Jayne says. "Kay-ira." "You don't need—we won't—but, oooh—"

My offer has smoothed over all this rough patch, and then—finally, finally, finally—she's kissing me. Her hand on my face again, her knuckles grazing my cheekbones, ever so softly. I inhale the scent of her hair—sweet, fall leaves with a hint of mint. And I let my forearm trace across her shoulder and down her back.

And then we're smart enough to go out to the alley to wait for James, which is a good thing, cuz I hear Mom and Sammie at the front door just as Jayne and I stumble out the back. Jayne lays her palm flat on my sternum. My heart flutters like a whiskey jack.

LESBO ALERT: [CENSORED]

CHAPTER
TWENTY-TWO

Jayne and I practically tumble into the back alley, our arms still wrapped around each other. Mind you, my house is close to the alley, and there's barely a strip of grass for our backyard, so we go from inside groping to outside smooching in record time. Alleys are great that way.

"Come to the dance tonight," I beg her without thinking.

This time, she's the one who pulls away. "You know I can't, Keira." And her voice sounds so full of regret. Because of *me*.

So I tug her ponytail loose, and her hair flaps around my forehead—slinky! "Come for one dance. Doesn't have to be a slow one. Two girls dancing together, just friends." I almost believe it can be that easy. That no one—not even Tyler—will think anything about us. Sita and I danced together at her sister's wedding, no big deal. "Girls danced with girls in junior high all the time. That's all your church friends will think is going on." I'm getting into this, now.

She actually laughs at me. We've had our first tiff, we've made it to the make-up make-out session, and my girlfriend (I have a girlfriend!) laughs at me. Her smile coils to the side.

"Your friends won't even notice!"

"Of course they won't, Keira." She sounds sarcastic.

"They won't! If two boys dance together, the world goes up in flames, but nobody ever cared when Sita and I danced together."

How easy it is to slip Sita's name into past tense! "Just one dance. I promise, I'll—"

She's laughing again. Her feet scuff some pebbles and she leans against our fence to wait for James. "Doofus," she zings at me. "Nobody from my church will think I'm a lesbian for dancing with a girl because nobody from my church will be at the dance." This *sounds* like great news, until she finishes: "Nobody from my church will be at the dance, because nobody from my church—*including me*—goes to dances. Ever. No exceptions. Finito."

"Oh," I say, my quick-witted comeback. This is a blow. This is yet another scratch at my already bruised and scraped heart, which jumped back into my body as soon as Jayne's lips touched mine. But I'm determined not to let Jayne see any surface scratches.

"It's okay," I tell her neck, which is where my lips have wandered. "We can dance right here. It's Hallowe'en. Two girls dancing in an alley can't be too weird, right?"

"What the HELL?!" So loud we jump away from each other. So loud the neighbours must think Trick-or-Treating has started early this year.

James.

He parked out front, then got out of his car and rang the bell when Jayne didn't come out. My mom sent him around back. Shite, did it look like we were kissing? We were dancing, but did it look like dancing, here in the daylight and without any music? Shit on a stick. Jayne's expression is a mixture of front page scandal and closed book. I try to deflect.

"It's Hallowe'en ..." I start, as if the day's name will work magic.

"Oh yeah? This some Satanic ritual?" James asks and jerks his head at us, as if performing some sort of ghoulish ceremony in a back alley makes more sense to him than dancing. Or maybe making fun of my inept cover-up.

"We were just fooling around," Jayne tells him, stepping away from me.

"Satan's funny to you?" James points his question at me. The good brother is gone; this James has "danger" scribbled all over his face, like all along he knew I'd be a bad friend for his sister, because he can't trust anyone outside his church community. Maybe he can't.

I straighten up, which makes me almost as tall as James. "No, sorry." I smile at him gently, like he's a wounded pet who needs convincing you won't hurt him. "No Satan, no rituals, no joke. Just two girls goofing around."

James doesn't look convinced. He isn't convinced. "You better stop," he says to me, and to Jayne: "Don't!" Then he grabs her arm, not hard, but as if he's trying to remind her who her real connections are, and he pulls her back along to the street where he's parked.

❋

Takes me ten minutes before I can force myself inside. I will not cry, I will not cry. In the house, it feels like the furnace is turned way down, but I fake being happy, because Mom's going to let me take Sam Trick-or-Treating, and she even lets us eat supper early, so Sam can hit the neighbourhood soon as the lip of the sun kisses the mountains.

"Get ready, get costumed, GO!" I yell from the entranceway,

waiting for Sam to dramatically wheel in. Even Mom looks happy as she piles mini-bars and cheapo-chips into a bowl by the front door. Sammie's Rubik's Cube costume is a big hit, but even I get compliments on my Pinball Wizard boots and diamond-studded goggles from *Tommy* (the '70s crack me up!). But you know what's wrong with the world? People!

We do our block and the next over. Mom says not to stay out past 7:30, but *come on*. The dance doesn't even start till eight, which means no one wants to be the first dweeb through the auditorium doors. So Sammie and I hold hands crossing the street and whip through the third block. She's got an edge over other kids cuz she can stash the heaviest candy in the pouch under her seat. And the farther we get from our own house, the more likely people will believe Sam's near-empty pumpkin-shaped bucket means she's only just started.

We roll up the sidewalk to the last house on the block. A woman holding a baby comes out in her PJs. The top is covered with a pattern of licorice allsorts bursting out of their boxes, and the bottoms have rows and rows of red and black licorice ropes. I think this is supposed to be the woman's costume, but maybe it's just whatever she had on this morning.

Sam holds out her once again nearly empty container and belts out, "Hallo-ween ap-pulls!"

The woman pours a handful of mini chocolate bars into Sam's orange pumpkin container. Score. We high-five and turn to go, but one of Sam's wheels gets stuck in a gaping cement crack in the driveway, and as I'm loosening her chair over the lip, I hear the woman call out: "You're so good with her."

"Excuse me?"

"Squeeze you, she doesn't even know you!" Sam throws out her favourite rejoinder.

"It's good of you to escort this crippled child on Hallowe'en." Pyjama woman doesn't know how to let go.

"Uh-oh," says Sammie.

"This *crippled child* is my *genius sister!*" I scream. "And *I'm* the one who needs an escort tonight, not *her*. Sammie here, she's ... she's the boss, she's the head-freakin-cheese!"

And I realize my anger is waaaay off the charts. No matter who I kiss or don't get to kiss any more, I'm Sammie's big sister, and I'm boiling over with sibling lava. I don't care that kids all over the street can hear me. That their parents will gleefully report this outburst to my parents. Great. Good. More grounding, more being forbidden to do any of the things that I'm not doing anyway. Sam's worth it. But as we roll down the sidewalk, I realize that my anger's also about Sita and Surge and Tyler and Jayne. And, oh yeah, about scaredy-cat me. No more later: *now*.

"Whew, *some*body's having an allergic reaction to those PJs," Sam chirps into her hand.

That kid really cracks me up.

❋

Guess we come in more quietly than I think, because when I go to the bathroom I hear Mom and Dad quarrelling in their bedroom. Long before bedtime, even.

"I tell you, Lenny, this girl's brother was *yelling* at them. Who knows what they were up to? But he yelled at them to stop." Oh, fabulous, the Mom Police overheard Brother Law.

"You worry too much, Alice. Keira's a *good* girl. Practically a ballerina!" Hmm—that's what my dad really thinks of my skating passion? "And ballerinas don't like other ballerinas, okay?"

"Maybe we shouldn't let her go to the dance. You ungrounded her too soon, even though she's offered no apology and no explanation for lying about the phone. Maybe we need to rethink that decision." My mother the backstabber.

"We can't ground her for no reason, darl." Yay, Dad! "Look, you told me this girl's family is religious, right?" Silence as my mom must be nodding. "Well, perhaps the brother doesn't think she should be friends with pagans."

"Lenny!" This time Dad gets a laugh out of Mom.

"Speaking of which, I have to hightail it to work to make sure all the devil-worshippers spend the night consuming copious amounts of their favourite devil brew."

And I hightail it to the kitchen, where I dutifully divide Sammie's spoils, so Mom can once-over the loot and give this candy haul the thumbs up.

"If you stay, you can steal my best loot," Sam pleads, but I leave the house as soon as Mom has Sam out of her costume and parked by the front door to greet late Trick-or-Treaters.

Suddenly, I'm burning to get to the dance. Burning to show up and flaunt my evil, single self. Because I deserve that, at least. I don't know what I mean by "at least," but I mean it wholeheartedly. Tyler's already left for the dance. Or so he'd told our parents. I'm pretty sure he went straight to party number one in a long list of parties he'd glide through tonight. Soon as Mom's attending to the twins from across the street dressed as Batgirl and Robin, I throw off my stilt-high boots, pull on my regular kicks, and head out.

The streets teem with movie characters and demons. I see a green blob and her ghostbuster and a cute pineapple milkshake, complete with rings of yellow covering her pigtails. These kids are awesome, I think, and wish I could snap a pic of them lined up with Sammie, but I pick up my pace and zoom toward Backstrom.

When I arrive, there are swarms of kids hanging out by the doors, leaning against the walls of the gym, crowding the giant speakers against the stage. With the exception of a few Goths (who just wear what they usually wear), and the zombie die-hards (get it? even grief-stricken, I crack me up), practically nobody's in costume. Most kids at Backstrom are too cool to play dress-up. Whatever. Makes it easier to spot who you're trying to avoid.

I catch a glimpse of Joline huddled with The Two, both wearing the "men-in-black" uniform, including cheesy sunglasses indoors (the '80s do *not* crack me up). Joline's wearing blue jean cut-offs with black nylons underneath and a floppy halter top. Cheap, yes? But where do I get off being a snob? Who the hell am I to preach about fashion?

I don't see Sita, and that should be a relief, that I don't have to suffer through her budding friendship with Talia, and her oh-so-out-in-the-open boy-girl relationship with Daz. Or Tony Baloney. Or whoever gets the role as the next Boy Number Lucky. Except: I'm done with relief. I'm done with being safe. I'm just mad that I'm finally in high school, finally know who I want, but I'm here all alone.

To be alone with my loneliness, I head for the girls' washroom. That's when I spot Amanda dancing with Daz. Uh-oh. Could be it's just one dance, but the look on Amanda's face says she hopes Sita comes by. She hopes Sita sees both of them hanging onto each other like that. I thought Amanda was coming to this dance with Titus. And what's Daz thinking? Or is he just dancing with his girlfriend's friend? Amanda sees me and waves a shimmering emerald sleeve at me furiously, like we're best friends, then she moves her hand lower on his back. Then even lower. She's smiling like she's doing all this for *me*, like I'm going to be happy that she's pissing off Sita. I dunno why, but Amanda being mean to Sita to get on my good side totally gets on my bad side.

Enough.

Enough, enough, enough.

I head over to the crowd of drama dweebs to see if Sita's hanging out with Daz's friends while he dances with another girl. Not Sita's style, but then again, maybe I don't know her style any more. She's not.

Next stop, the girl's washroom. But it's crowded with girls blowing their curls, re-applying lipstick, tracing black lines under their eyes. No costumes, just the regular girl disguises. Next, I try the bathroom on the second floor. Fewer girls, but almost as much perfume, so I head up two more levels. On the fourth floor, I'm amazed to see Sita at her locker. Or rather, I see an open locker, with Sita's legs below the locker door. So I walk up and start to talk to her locker door, because that seems to be the only way we talk now.

"Sita, I'm sorry. I really am sorry. For not telling you earlier, for not telling you the right way, for not sending that text message earlier. But not ... not for being attracted to girls." I sort of get scared saying this. "Or both girls and boys. Or whatever. I'm ... whatever, okay? *Okay?*"

What if this really is it? What if Sita cannot take me for who I am? I gulp and keep going. "And I'm sorry I freaked out telling you. I don't know what I am most of the time. But I know I'm your friend. And it shouldn't matter who we kiss, as long as we always tell each other about it, right? Right? *Right?!*"

The locker door stays open, blocking my face from hers. I don't know what else to say. If the only other thing I can say to make Sita forgive me is to take all of myself back, then I guess we won't be friends any more. I can't stand that. I'm ready to grovel, but—after everything that's happened this week—I can't put myself back inside any box.

Sita slams her locker door shut and with such force that I almost walk away, but I see that she's crying. Not relief tears, not dainty droplets on her cheek because we've finally made up; this is huge, grief-stricken panic weeping.

"I slept with Lucien!" she blubbers. Yikes to the nth degree!

And then I get the whole story of Sita's rough patch. After I ran away from our Lactose Tolerant conversation, she *was* a bit freaked out. She'd asked me if I liked girls because she suspected me, because I never seem interested enough in boys. But she *was* half hoping I'd just reassure her to the contrary. Then, when I didn't and screamed at her that no way would I ever want to kiss her, and said that maybe *she* was curious about me for some reason—

"I did *not* say that," but I'm smiling at her, not chastising. I need to listen to Sita's story right now. All this time, *she's* been needing a friend.

"Well, there you were," she sniffs, "telling me that kissing a boy turned you into a lesbian or something, and maybe that meant you wanted me to be one too, except I'm apparently too repulsive to kiss" (she hand-waves to show she's teasing). Sita's story is going all over the place, but it doesn't matter. Not any more. She's talking to me; we're back together again. "So I texted Daz, and when he called back, I blubbered a bit, but wouldn't tell him why because I didn't know if you'd told me to keep this a secret, so we had another fight, this one about me keeping things from him. And—" the tears start pouring down her face, "he dumped me. Again. Over the phone. And, and, and...!" She's crying again, so I pull her over to a window ledge where we can sit and view the latecomers arriving outside and still enjoy some cone-of-silence privacy.

"And then he called me a *slut*." Somehow, saying that word out loud about herself calms Sita. Maybe because this means Daz isn't worth crying over? I hope so.

And then, she tells me, despite older sisters who have warned her and warned her and warned her about the wild-animal zoo-trip that is high school dating, Sita rushed over to Lucien's. "And I practically jumped at his invitation to hop into—"

"—bed with him?"

"Couch, actually," she corrects. "His mom wasn't due home for hours, and my parents knew I'd be with you all evening."

Sita's first time going all the way, and it's revenge sex. She's bawling now, and I get it. Not only did Sita screw up, but she screwed up in a colossally un-Sita-like way. She's the one who only kisses or feels a boy up or lets a boy grab her private parts if she wants to. Never just because *they* want to. But she was so furious at Daz that she flew into another boy's lap, just to prove him right.

Sita and I haven't talked for weeks, so most of it comes out in a jumble. When I didn't have her to talk to, it seemed like the days slowed down to mush-speed. But as soon as we hug, the world speeds up again. At some point, Sita will give me more details. But right now, I hug her and hug her some more.

"Let's get out of here, okay?" I say. I don't need to be at the dance any more, not if I can hang out with Sita. "Your place, my place, or just walking. There were some pretty good ghouls out before. Some of our neighbours went ballistic with the creaky coffins and floating ghosts. And Sam will let you steal her best chocolate bars."

Sita nods and gets up, but adds, "I have to say goodbye to Talia. We came together."

Oh. My heart does slam into the floorboards at that. But Sita deserves friends right now, as many as she wants. "Sure, I saw her dancing when I walked through the gym earlier." And I tell her, "I was looking for you," to make her realize she's the one who's important. That me stumbling across her standing at her locker wasn't an accidental meeting.

"Yeah, I talked to Talia about Lucien." Sita hand-waves. "Not that she had great advice, but at least I could tell somebody. With you AWOL ..."

Now Sita doesn't have to explain becoming friends with Talia Sitkins. Why would I think I'm the only one with a calamitous love life? The two of us practically run down the steps together and toward the auditorium.

"By the way, I really never did get the text message you were talking about," she tells me as we enter the gym. "You think I would have ignored an apology?"

But I was so sure I pressed "send." I saw the little bars fill up the screen. Which is why I figured I had a right to be angry at Sita for not responding, for being too mean to accept my apology. My one measly apology. That, apparently, I never even managed to send.

But just as I'm about to delve into mega-mea-culpa mode, the curtains part, the spotlight goes on, the music swells. Okay, none of these things happen, but I *do* suddenly spot Jayne across the dance floor. Standing there looking soooo like a sore thumb.

I grab Sita's shoulder and squeeze it hard. "Um, there's something else I have to tell you," I blurt out, just as—

"*Keira!*" A voice booms louder than the speakers, booming out to everyone on the dance floor. A guy sporting a hand-drawn pirate patch is running toward me.

On the ice, I can leap too wide during a jump and land slightly off-target, knowing I won't have left myself enough room for the spin that comes next in my routine. But in the fractured second it takes to feel my body a few centimetres too close to the boards, I can adjust. I can add a three-turn or skate backwards or add extra crossover steps, then tighten the spin so I don't lose any time, don't miss a beat. Not on this dance floor.

Surge. Here. Running toward me. Surging toward me. And I suddenly realize his name isn't Surge, but Serge, a traditional French name, not a goofy boy's nickname. I say it out loud: "Serge."

He plants a kiss on my lips. This is a crazy world, where church girls attend banned dances and boys who live way north of Edmonton appear in the middle of Calgary. And my best friend Sita doesn't know two things about this person I'm kissing and even less about the person I *wish* I could be kissing.

Jayne.

When I pull back from Serge's lips, I don't see her any more. Literally pushing past his lips, I leave him to fend for himself.

"Sorry ... I'm sorry," I say, but aim my words at the spot where Jayne stood. I feel terrible that Serge has come here, for me, and I'm running away from him. But I have to find Jayne right now; I'll come back and deal with this mess after I catch up with Jayne and try to deal with that mess first.

❋

Sita tells me later that Serge is the one who got my text (when I wrote that apology message, I missed by one letter under "S"). He texted back umpteen times, but Mom had my phone locked up by then. When I didn't answer, he decided a grand gesture was called for. Serge skipped school so he could hop a bus to Edmonton and then another bus to Calgary. Took him over six hours. On the way, he sent me a swack of texts, telling me he knew my school had a Hallowe'en dance that day, and I should definitely go because there'd be a surprise there for me.

As Sita said, "Thank Shiva your mom didn't sneak peeks at your messages." Although if she had, getting grounded would have been so much less terrible than everything else that happened. Once on the bus, Serge worried that he'd run out of the house without a costume. So he drew a cheesy moustache-beard combo on his face and coloured in a patch over his eye with a black marker. Then he wound a pink cloth napkin around his head that he swiped from a truck stop in Red Deer. And a binder ring he'd clipped to his left ear.

By the time Sita told me all these details, it was way too late to call him, to thank him for making the trip down, just for me. And way too late to apologize. Serge took the red-eye bus back and must have arrived home around five in the morning.

But at the dance, Sita saw a boy kiss me, saw me withdraw from the boy's arms and run past him, and did the math. As I ran for the doors, she pulled Serge in the other direction. She dragged him out into the goblin-filled night, and then he let her walk him back to the bus depot. Sita shoved him toward the bathroom to wash his face and got in line for him. She bought his ticket, she bought him a sandwich at the kiosk, she bought him a motorcycle magazine to read on the bus. We'd been friends again for less than an hour, yet Sita took charge of my mess of a love life and fixed up as much of it as she could. Which means she missed everything that happened next:

Jayne running through the parking lot, and me spotting her as I burst out the double doors, even though it's lightly snowing. How did she get to the dance, what lie did she have to tell her family to get here? Maybe she convinced James to drive her, "just for a minute, just for a second," just to "straighten Keira out," or maybe she simply sneaked out of the house to be with me at the dance.

Then I see his car. James gets out and waves Jayne over. He starts toward her.

Without thinking, I call out, "No, *he* kissed *me!* Please, Jayne, I didn't kiss him!" My feet think they're on skates; I've somehow tricked them into thinking we're already at tomorrow's competition, so they glide me across the snowy asphalt in record time. My breathing comes out in shards, and what's left of my heart pounds into my ribs, but my legs get me there.

I call out again, "Jayne, wait! Jayne, I'm sorry!" but either she doesn't hear me or sorry isn't enough.

I don't blame her. Until today, I was too petrified to hold her hand in public, but I'll apparently kiss any old boy in front of every student in the school.

James's arm around Jayne's shoulders, they walk away from me. I should be the one with my arm around her shoulders, not the one who makes her need an arm there.

"I wasn't kissing him, Jayne!" I sob. "Please, stop!"

When they get to the car, James hugs her, calms her down. He's being the protective big brother, protecting Jayne from awful me. When I reach them, I try to see if she's crying or devastated or just angry, but Jayne keeps her face turned away from me. My breath is so jagged, it seems to fill the parking lot. James opens the back door, and I think she's going to crawl in without even talking to me, but she hesitates, and both James and I notice. Every molecule in my body lifts when Jayne doesn't just disappear into that car.

Still rasping air, I touch Jayne's arm so I don't have to apologize to the back of her head. She turns, and I see her eyes are red. She's hurting. Because of me. *I can fix this. I'm so going to fix this.*

James reaches down, grabs something from the backseat. Then he takes a step toward me, his face an earthquake, an eruption of bile. In a flash, he shoots out his hand as if to shake mine. No alert, no alarm, just his fist moving too fast, blazing bright, shimmering in the light from the open car door—

—and then all I feel is a tremendous anguish in my belly, like James has punched me. Like my heart's been broken and stomped on, but my heart's in the wrong place. A very, very wrong place. Jayne makes a funny noise—not funny like laughing, but like the gulping sound our fridge sometimes makes—when James stabs me.

And then nothing.

CHAPTER: THE END

I wake up and the first thing I feel is the all-encompassing damage that I used to call my body. One eyelid, then the other. I'm alone in a hospital room.

I try to figure out what's going on: I have bandages on my belly and up the back of my right leg. I'm attached to an IV. I don't remember getting hit in the leg, but then, once James's hand congealed into a knife, I just felt absolute agony and passed out.

Which means that at some point James stopped stabbing me and someone called an ambulance. Oh yeah, I remember waking up in the ambulance and twice more on a gurney in the middle of the hospital hallway. Each time, a voice asked me my name and each time, a sharp, horrific pain ripped through me. And each time, I passed out again.

This time, when I wake up, I can't locate the pain in any one specific place. So I try to sit up, and feel that same rip of anguish in my stomach, as if to let me know that whatever happened really happened.

"Keira!" Mom rushes in. "Don't move, baby, you just keep lying there." Behind my mom, Tyler, poking his head into the room. His mouth contorts and he tosses a box of chocolates onto the bed. Tyler leans his head past the doorway, but his feet stay out. In a moment, even his head disappears.

Mom pulls a chair right up to the bed's edge and rests one hand on the metal frame. She rests her other hand on my forehead, like having a fever might be the worst of my problems. She doesn't speak. Beeps come from a nearby room, a plane flies directly above the hospital, I can hear someone pacing the hall. Maybe nurses. Maybe Tyler. If Tyler's here, I must be dying.

The doctor comes in and informs me that James's knife went into my abdomen, but not very far. Didn't even cut through my stomach, just hurt like a skate blade in my gut, pick first. All I have to do now is wait for the stitches to do their work, lie around *a lot*, and I'll be fine. Those are the doctor's exact words: "You're fine, there's little wrong with you that time won't heal."

Turns out I have a bandage on my right leg because—after I went down from the gut thrust—James bent down to hamstring me, but he missed. Still, the knife tore through my calf tissue, leaving me with a serious avulsion injury (Winnie's worst fear). How messed up do you have to be to attack another person, like, surgically?

Once home, I'll be confined to my bed for two weeks, then I'll hobble for three or four weeks on crutches, and then limp for months after that. Maybe longer. My right leg feels weird, sore and awkward and detached from the rest of me. Maybe I'll limp right into grade eleven, or even graduation. For right now, I need a nurse just to get to the bathroom. Mostly, I pass out a lot.

When I wake up again, Mom's still by my bed. At some point, she'll demand to know what I did to deserve being stabbed. Do I have an answer?

Instead, I stick to a safe topic. "Where's Dad?" I ask. Mom reaches for my hand, but doesn't answer. "Is he at work? Wait, what time is it?" The pale light drifting through the window feels like evening. Is it tomorrow night? Who's taking care of Sam?

Mom smooths the hospital sheets that I've bunched in my fist. My head hurts just from trying to figure out what time of day it is, and I didn't even get stabbed in the head. Holy shit! Did he cut my *head*? My hands jolt to my skull to check for scarring, and I nearly puke from the pain.

Okay, Dad usually sleeps in, in the morning, but ... I can't figure it out. Too many questions, most of which I'm not about to ask Mom. Like: should I call Serge or will I only make him feel worse? "So, am I trapped in here, am I on some kind of danger alert? Or are they gonna let me out with a warning?" I'm trying to come off as adorable, as brave and funny. Every muscle hurts, but I don't pass out. "And Sam? You guys didn't tell—"

"Samantha's at a play date," Mom informs me. "Tyler will pick her up in a few hours."

"So Dad's working early ...?" My tongue stumbles: "Or he—

Mom cuts in, "Keira." Full stop. Tyler's left shoulder leans against the door jam. I hear the ping of an elevator and other droning hallway noises. Mom tries her own deep breath trick. "Your dad and I ... we disagree. About what ... about you."

My heart sinks, slithers.

"He ... he doesn't want you to come home." Before my heart can take another blow, she jumps in: "He's upset, he's just blaring and buzzing." Mom's palm against my face stroking and bolstering my deteriorating centre. "Your home is your home, of course, and you belong at home." Now it's her tongue that doesn't work properly.

My whole body blubbers.

"Oh, Keira. Oh, baby." A few of her own tears peek out. "Tyler and I told him he can't"—she swallows—"keep you from your home. For now, he's staying at the hotel where he works in the bar. He'll cool off."

"Dad doesn't want me ... doesn't want me home?" I ask. All the skating falls I've ever experienced have never made me hurt like this. My funny-brave mask cracks open, and I can't think of a single cute response. I am over-the-top sob-heaving when Mom scoots over and gently pulls my head into her arms. She holds me like I'm her baby, and then we're bawling together.

✳

I could have spent the rest of my high school years as a het-girl. I could have saved the gay pride parade for after I'm past the parental grip. That's how Jayne planned to do it.

But I would do it all again. Most of it. The kissing a girl part, the still liking (some) boys. Jayne's wrong about me; I do know who I am, I just don't have a dictionary definition. My body's a mess, my brain's jumbled, but I'm not confused, not any more. I try to hold onto that, that I know who I am. I try to clutch that thought permanently between my fingers and squeeze. When I do, Mom just sees me clenching the sheets.

Mom has barely left my room since our Big Cry. Tyler brings Sam—who loves racing up and down hospital ramps, and adores that she and I wheelchair it to the visiting lounge together—and he takes her home at night. When he's around, Tyler's expression zips around like a rollercoaster, though he mostly just stays away. But when Mom gets up to pee, he leans into the room and tosses a key onto the bed.

"Mom told Dad we changed the locks," he explains, as if that clears everything up. And in a way, it does. I can't imagine Dad knocking on the door to his own house, but I can't picture him trying to bust in, either.

❋

The greatest casualty is that I can't skate. Not in the finals, not in any upcoming competition, not even for fun. Technically, I can *skate*, but the doctor explains that my right leg can't bear to *land*.

I ask about the competition. Mom says that Zoë Bandicoff came in first, perfectly primed for the Provincials in January. I ask the doctor how long I'll have to be away from skating practice. If I could manage four weeks over the summer, I can get back into form after six weeks off my feet, right?

"No skating," the doctor tells me, and heads out to finish rounds. I slump down in my bed. My legs slump with me. "No skating" is also what the physio tells me when she comes round to explain my exercises. What Mom repeatedly tells me, what all the nurses tell me. Mom admits that Winnie pulled my name from the application roster for the Provincials as soon as Mom called her. No more ice for Keira. By the time my leg recovers, *if* it recovers, the competitions will have left me behind. No more skating—sounds like a sentence out of a science-fiction novel, to me. No lights, no music, no trophy. No *fun*. Every time my throbbing leg wakes me up, I cry. How can I lose skating too? Truth be true, this loss hurts more than losing Jayne. When I fall asleep, I dream I'm in the Finals, executing a perfect triple Lutz, but when I land my blade collapses, my toe smashes through the ice, and my leg disappears underneath me.

The one thing I was good at, really good at, and James took that from me, too.

BI ALERT: *WITHIN MINUTES—KISSES A BOY, DECLARES LOVE TO A GIRL, DUMPS THE BOY, REUNITES WITH HER BFF.*

POST-TRAUMATIC EPILOGUE SYNDROME

First day she visits, Sita tells me all about Serge and more about what everyone's now calling "the incident." I learn that Jayne wasn't the one who called the ambulance. Joline called them. She came out of the school doors behind me, probably to sneak a smoke. Then she saw me go down like I was punched. She dialled 9-1-1, and yelled, "I'm calling 9-1-1! I'm calling 9-1-1!" as she flew across the parking lot. *Joline*, my saviour.

James got the hell out of there. "So did the other girl," Mom adds. She still won't leave my room, she can barely stop holding my hand. She says "the other girl," like Jayne's not part of what happened to me. I don't push it, though; it's not like I told Mom anything about Jayne before Hallowe'en. The cops arrested James the very evening of the attack—he was at home. And he's been arraigned already. He acted ruthlessly to save his sister from evil me. Sita whispers that last part.

My hospital room fills with get-well cards and boxes and boxes of candy. The cards include: a pop-up thermometer from Marisol and Raf; a non-descript paisley card from the school principal and staff; a giant cardboard skate signed by Winnie and Zoë and all my skating pals. Joline and The Two, Marly and Kaitlyn, even sent cards. And Sita's family's been sending over paneer pakora snacks and raisin and nut naan bread practically every day.

Nothing from Dad, though I overheard Mom crying into the phone last night when she thought I was long asleep.

Tyler buys me a T-shirt that he leaves on my bed while I'm out of the room doing a hospital lap with Sammie. It reads: "Favourite Parent: Praying Mantis." Tyler. Who tortured me for years, but in a sibling way. Maybe we don't hate each other, I think, now that I've seen what hate really looks like. Maybe we just haven't learned how to be regular people with each other.

"Why did she leave?" I ask Sita, when my Mom's finally taken the hint and offers to pick Sam up from school while Tyler goes to basketball practice. Sita knows exactly what I'm asking and what the right answer should be. But after all we've been through, Sita isn't going to candy-coat what happened.

"I dunno, Keira," she says. No actual hand-flip, but it's in her voice.

Me, I can't let it go. "She went with James. She chose him." Of all the things I feared, when it came to getting close to a girl, her choosing her violent brother over me wasn't one of them. "She stood right there when the knife went in—" I choke, but I keep going. "She saw me go down. She saw my blood."

"She probably froze," Sita says. "She froze because it was so scary and unbelievable." She takes a breath, and then out come all her theories, like she's been asking herself the same question and so can give me answers. "She froze, or she panicked. Or she's afraid of James, who's a crazy maniac. But the real answer—who knows? From what you say, Jayne seemed like good people, but you didn't know her very well."

Sita's not blaming me, but I realize that I really didn't know the only two people I've ever kissed. How bad is that?

"Okay, um, not sure how to tell you, but it gets worse," she warns me.

I clench the sheets, as if that'll help. "How can it get worse than being stabbed by my girlfriend's maniac brother?"

"Her dad sent her away."

"Away," I repeat. "Where away? For how long?"

"For forever," Sita answers. "The neighbour on our right goes to Jayne's family's church. She reported to my mother all about Jayne's dad putting an end to her heathen life here in the big city." Sita takes a breath and gets to the roughest patch of her story. "Jayne's dad sent her to a religious school in the middle of nowhere, and he asked them to bump her back to grade nine. He said she needs the time to mature, but he obviously just wants her in jail for as long as possible." Sita strokes my arm. "She's not coming back, Keira. They're not allowed phones or computers there. They even have a dress code."

And that tiny detail is somehow the last straw because then I picture Jayne in a flowery print dress instead of her decorated jeans. And now I can't see her face any more, which makes me burst into tears. Again.

"They'll probably make her change the spelling of her name," I sputter, like her fading into a real Plain Jane is the worst tragedy ever. I cry out a bathtub of tears, then I cry out the entire Bow River, and then the Elbow River for good measure. And when I'm done, Sita wipes my eyes with her sleeve.

❋

Getting knifed pretty much put an end to everything that matters to me: skating and competitive finals. Having a girlfriend. Oh, and managing to stay in the closet.

Sita tells me that "the incident" is Backstrom's latest hot topic. So much for me sinking back into invisible dorkdom when I finally get back to school. Sita says the cafeteria literally buzzes with comments about how I've been knifed for being queer. "And Oh-Em-Gawd, Keira, when Jason Billings brayed out 'Keira-the-lezzie' right in the middle of assembly, *three* of his jock pals stood up and yanked him to the floor. And not gently." Sita's happy to report any hostility toward Jason-the-Pillings. But who cares what other kids think? I'm me, now. At last, just me. Here to stay.

Sita shows up every frigging afternoon and tells me funny stories about Drama Club dress rehearsal malfunctions and mandatory school assemblies. "Amanda has disappeared from our lunch table, but whether it's because you might be contagious or because I am, who knows?" Sita grins wickedly. "More room for Daz. And your crutches, when you join us."

Yep, Daz. After the noisy dance kissing, Daz and Amanda parted bodies for good. Sita and he performed out-and-out mutual forgiveness, and now live deep within make-up land. While Sita tells me stories, he covers for her in Drama Club, and texts her info about their next play (a stage version of *Hitchhiker's Guide to the Galaxy*—harmless, funny, and safely set in the future). She flirts with Daz on the phone when he can hear I'm right there, and now sometimes even flirts with me.

I don't know how she does it, exactly. I get violently yanked out of the half-way closet, and she's already able to make light of everyone's sexuality *and* flirt in non-threatening ways, *and* reassure me that she's not freaking out that I'm going to jump her just because my lesbo-insides have trumped my het-instincts. No wonder boys fall for her. No wonder Daz falls for her all over again.

⁂

Today I get to go home. Mom's over by the window, arranging more flowers. I hear Tyler and Sam in the hallway, spinning. "He's a right shit-for-brains," I hear Tyler say to Sammie when she asks him when Dad's coming to the hospital. Will Dad be at home when we get there? Will he still be gone? My belly clenches at both the image of Dad at the table with his newspapers spread all around him, and him not there at all—a family photo with a Dad-hole smack in the middle. Sam rolls up to my hospital bed and strokes my arm with one hand, brandishing a deck of cards with the other.

"You *have* figured out that I cheat at Cheat, right?" she asks, pulling my food tray closer. "I'm dealing in everyone because Tyler will get in here if we make him, and the Mom Police will play, too."

Sponge-alert! "Sam, it's time to retire that nickname." Especially since I definitely prefer a concerned cop-like parent to a father who could only fake being Lenient Lenny. I've figured out that Dad was a benevolent dictator: he didn't have to enforce the rules because things usually went his way. It's why he didn't want to admit my Jayne-related inclinations. As long as he didn't talk about it, his daughter stayed too young and innocent to be a freak. But as soon as I got attacked, he couldn't glide over my awkward soul any more.

Sammie's finished dealing the whole deck. "Pay attention, Keira. Cheating is how come I always win. And it *is* the point of the game." We both laugh just as Mom returns from a pizza run.

"Come join," I invite her. She's never played cards with us, not even when we're on vacation. Because she's always too busy working overtime or cooking healthy meals, or because we've never asked her?

"Come on, I'll teach you the rules." I gingerly sit up. My gut throbs, but it's not unbearable.

"Except none of the rules matter," I say. "You can cheat as much as you want, as long as nobody catches you." Mom sits down and pulls Tyler in beside her. We each grab a slice and awkwardly hold our cards in one hand and spicy pizza in another. "But I should warn you, Mom, no matter what play you pull off, Sammie always wins." And I wink at Sam, who shrugs at Mom, as if she doesn't know what I'm talking about.

On the good news front, Joline and I are actually friends now. Really friends, not just sit-together-because-our-mothers-think-we-should friends. She calls me and we text (Mom brought in my phone). Joline even showed up one afternoon when Sita really couldn't afford to miss another rehearsal and hung out until—as she said—"it was time to limp home" (yes, she still mocks me). Hey, the girl saved me,

I think I can manage to like her just a teeny bit. When I thank her and tell her how grateful I am that she was around that night, she says, "Okay, but I don't want any lezzie-germs rubbing off on me." For a second I think she's serious, but it's such a ridic thing to say we both burst into hysterics. We make arrangements to meet at the mall once my legs are crutch-worthy, and maybe catch an afternoon matinee. "Hey, and with your crutches, maybe we can get a disability discount, too, eh?" The girl doesn't know how to stop when she's behind.

Sita might not like that she has sarcasm competition, I think, but it's amazing how far being an invalid will get you these days. Ha, now I'm doing it. My leg hurts, my stomach hurts, my girlfriend has been literally wrenched out of my life. The Olympic dream is now just the stuff of dreams. But as I reach for my phone, I can't help but shake my head.

"Ridic," I text to Sita, "life is ab-scama-lute-ly ridic."

SEQUEL ALERT: *HIGH SCHOOL—ONLY 2.7 YEARS TO GO...*

ACKNOWLEDGMENTS

So many people help bring a book together, some through direct involvement and some through tangential splendour, and this book is no exception.

Thanks to Susan Holloway and Joa Markotić for graciously providing info and details about Junior Rangers, to Rosemary Nixon for suggestively rebuffing my pleas to co-write a kid's book, to Susan Holbrook for sharing a constant state of overwhelmedness, and to Louis Cabri for living with "panic" during the early, okay, also the middle, and certainly the final months of this manuscript!

I worked on a first draft when I lived in Australia for a few months, and I thank Leigh Dale as well as numerous faculty and staff at the University of Wollongong for offering administrative support and assistance, library access, and all manners of pleasant bookish exchanges.

I massively thank Debra Dudek for tremendous help integrating, acclimatizing, and navigating the Wollongong campus and surrounding areas, and for her brilliant advice on book titles and local wineries.

Writer Glen Huser gave me valuable early commentary, and I thank him for his overall wit, his smarts about YA books, and for his astute suggestions.

The Thor allusion on page 104 is thanks to Catriona Strang and Nina Houle, and the monster joke on page 139 is thanks to Zorien Markotić.

Endless thanks to the entire Arsenal team: Brian Lam for wanting this manuscript, Oliver McPartlin for designing such a terrific cover, Cynara Geissler for her marketing and publicity skills, and all others who helped this book along the way. Most notably, I thank and thank and thank Susan Safyan, for her keen eye, for her editing skill, and for her delicate determination to hack away at all my cheese!

Photo: Don Denton

Nicole Markotić is a novelist, critic, and poet who teaches Children's Literature and Creative Writing at the University of Windsor. She has widely published in Canada, the USA, Australia, and Europe; her most recent book is the poetry collection *Whelmed* (Coach House). She works as a fiction and poetry editor and publishes a chapbook series under Wrinkle Press. Her previous book with Arsenal Pulp Press is the novel *Scrapbook of My Years as a Zealot*.